Sleeping Alone

Sleeping Alone

Stories

Ru Freeman

Graywolf Press

Versions of the following stories were first published in:
World Literature Today: "First Son"
Writecorner: "What Could Be Said about Pedris Road"
VQR: "Sleeping Alone"
Kriti: "Beauty Treatments"
StoryQuarterly: "The Irish Girl"
Michigan Quarterly Review: "Retaining Walls"
Delmarva Review: "The Bridge"
Guernica: "Matthew's Story"
Tales of Two Americas: Stories of Inequality in a Divided Nation
    (John Freeman, ed.): "Fault Lines"

This publication is made possible, in part, by the voters of Minnesota through a Minnesota State Arts Board Operating Support grant, thanks to a legislative appropriation from the arts and cultural heritage fund. Significant support has also been provided by the McKnight Foundation, the Lannan Foundation, the Amazon Literary Partnership, and other generous contributions from foundations, corporations, and individuals. To these organizations and individuals we offer our heartfelt thanks.

MINNESOTA
STATE ARTS BOARD

CLEAN
WATER
LAND &
LEGACY
AMENDMENT

Published by Graywolf Press
212 Third Avenue North, Suite 485
Minneapolis, Minnesota 55401

All rights reserved.

www.graywolfpress.org

Published in the United States of America
Printed in Canada

ISBN 978-1-64445-088-8 (paperback)
ISBN 978-1-64445-176-2 (ebook)

2 4 6 8 9 7 5 3 1
First Graywolf Printing, 2022

Library of Congress Control Number: 2021945916

Cover design: Kimberly Glyder

Cover art: Miguel Sotomayor / Moment / Getty Images (kites);
        Shutterstock (tape)

For my daughters
Duránya, Hasadrī, & Kisārā

—

May you always find the stories
behind the ones you hear

Contents

Sleeping Alone

The Wake

What is truth? This is: Oric Boyar, a former actor, astrologist, voice coach, and charismatic cult leader, convinced his followers to help raise a dead man to life in a New York City apartment, keeping vigil over the decomposing corpse for two months.

—

The cult, which is what her father called it, and which term she herself feared it deserved, met every week now and only in the Swastika bedroom that she shared with her brother; which is why the corpse also had to lie there.

"Agapito says that this is the only room in which he has felt the divine vibrancies in the whole of New York," Rene, her mother, said on one of the early days.

Did he mean the whole of New York or only the city? And if it was the city alone, did it encompass the boroughs? Had he been in every loft and tenement? Her mother turned away from such questions, particularly when uttered by a husband who had already broken the only butter rule.

"Agapito says that we must eat no fish, flesh, or fowl and we must cook only with butter," Rene had announced one morning. Sylvia, her brother, and their father watched while a week's worth of good groceries went down the garbage chute rigged ingeniously inside the dumbwaiter.

"That is kosher meat!" her father said. Kosher was her father's equivalent of organic. They were not Jewish. Perhaps being the only Italian family in a building full of Jewish families had been the genesis of this preference. Still, despite the considerable pride he displayed whenever he came home having secured some past-best-before from The Kosher Marketplace, he didn't move to stop the waste. He rarely moved to stop her mother from anything, not even the construction of the Swastika Room, which is where she and her brother unfolded day by day. In truth, it fell far short of a real swastika, but her brother, Dickens, had insisted on the name.

"We are the Jews in this family," he had said to Sylvia. "Those two are living life while you and I are merely surviving." Dickens had discovered bitterness when he turned twelve and he was relentless about airing it with a certain theatrical flair.

She understood, Sylvia did, in her forgiving way, that the sleeping arrangement was a necessary innovation. She had been reminded, quite often, that their apartment in Manhattan was both an asset and a mousehole, and that was after her parents had "moved up" and away from the crumbling wasteland of legend and fall that had been their old place: the Marple Tower on Fifty-Seventh Street. And although this move had predated her birth, that history had imbued Sylvia with a certain gravitas that caused her to be zealously grateful for space.

"They need privacy," Rene said, a relatively short sentence for her, as she tore out the sheet of linen paper that she usually reserved for unnecessarily long thank-you notes written in exquisite calligraphy for correspondingly insignificant gifts: a cup of coffee after school with another mother perhaps, or a bag of apples from a dark-skinned student in the fall. She sketched the design in blue Biro.

Dickens had been unimpressed. "We're going to be in a prison, Syl, that's all it is. A prison."

But prison or not, their father hauled lumber up in the same dumbwaiter, the trash held back for a day, and went to work. When he hammered and nailed and grunted and yelped inside their thirty-by-twenty-foot room, Sylvia was disturbed less by the hammering than by the yelps. For a baritone whose voice was his profession, yelps were not becoming. She winced and made untenable promises to unknown deities to spare him the loss of his voice, while her mother paced outside, as though this would hasten completion of the task.

Her mother was a riddle that Sylvia was determined to solve.

Rene, by her frequent account over dinners when her husband was not in attendance, had married into the ephemera of talent and popularity. Sylvia's father, Sansone, had been thirty-five years old and distinguished in the world of independent musical theater, complete with a seasonal directorship at an upstate summer camp for kids with a thirst for the stage. In the eyes of nineteen-year-old Rene, Sansone had seemed a most prudent choice, his professional qualifications only enhanced by the numerous women who lingered at his side. Surely, if he chose her, it had to have been because she presented, and he recognized, a combination of musical gift and youthful beauty in her that surpassed anything or, for that matter, anyone he could commandeer to his side. It was far too late when she realized it had been nothing more than love. By then, Dickens was born, and Sylvia incubating.

Indeed, everything Rene had done thus far had been either a statement of past regret or a mysterious wager made in the name of a better future. One in which she, through dint of desire and purchase, if not nature, would acquire the ability to breathe, project, and gain flexibility in her voice to rival that which had unfairly come to life along with her husband at his birth, through no effort of his. Yet musical comedy, folk, and Italian art song classes, endless stints as the inglorious second soprano at various community events, and even the expensive theory teacher who had introduced her to the concept of oratorio and cajoled her into joining the Presbyterian church choir had failed to achieve anything more than frustration. One spring, when Sylvia was just five and Dickens seven, Rene had spent a whole month dragging them to Verdi Square every morning at 6:00 to gaze for a full fifteen minutes, timed by her gold wristwatch, at the statue of Giuseppe Verdi and each of the other four characters whom Sylvia grew to know only in later years as Falstaff, Leonora, Aida, and Otello but at the time had assumed, since she and Dickens were forced to attend this ritual, were Verdi's adult children. It had been during a long period when her parents were not speaking to each other and Sylvia had feared, additionally, that her mother was praying that her husband and children would be turned into stone.

In the scheme of things, therefore, Sylvia felt that being asked to sleep for a month on the floor of the living room between the orange fold-out couch that their parents made up each night and the reflective Steinway grand that was her mother's tool of trade, while her father made a life-sized magic box out of their room was entirely within reason. She entertained herself by imagining that they were on a stage, a feeling enhanced by the deep purple drapes that her mother had hung from ceiling to floor; drapes that had never been drawn but simply stood, like rippled pillars on either side of the orange couch. The drapes, hanging thus in Apt. 19G on 909 West Seventy-Ninth Street, which address, Sylvia felt, had a likable cadence to it, convinced her that it was not beyond the realm of possibility that she might wake from a dream to find herself in midperformance in a theater made luminous by adoring fans. The vision helped her fall asleep.

—

The grand opening occurred on a Friday in June, which fell thirty days on each end from her eleventh birthday and her brother's thirteenth one.

On Fridays, they always cooked real food. Food that her mother purchased on Thursdays at *The* Indian Grocery. For their celebratory dinner, her mother simmered fresh vegetables in coconut milk, which she served with semolina cooked and sliced into wedges. Dessert was rice pudding made without milk. The crushed kernels floated along with sugared pistachios and slivered almonds and very small raisins in a broth made entirely of butter. Afterward, the room.

"Happy birthday!" her father exclaimed, removing his palms from over her eyes. Before her was a sharp-edged S-shaped platform that fit neatly right into the center of their room. There was about four feet of space between the bottom edge of the S and the floor and a similar gap between the top edge and the ceiling. The vertical middle was broken up by a smooth square hole accessed by a short ladder consisting of two steps.

"Happy birthday!" her mother echoed, removing her palms from Dickens's face.

"See? Sylvia, your mattress is under here, under this plank, which is also the floor for your brother's room," her father said, making quotation marks with his fingers as he said that, "room." "Dickens, when you get off your mattress, which is on the top right-hand side, you will be able to stand straight up! Just don't jump on it. You don't want to crack the wood."

Perhaps the fact that he might land on her sleeping face was too gruesome to contemplate, Sylvia thought. She was grateful for this salient consideration.

"And," her father continued, "you, my dear, can stand up on this side." He moved in a Fred Astaire twist-footed dance to the right side of the room, taking her by the hand as he did so. Sylvia stood on the long side of her "room" and looked up at the platform where, she assumed, Dickens would eventually be sleeping. Her father explained further, "You can put your desk at one end, your bureau at the other end and still have standing room."

"How do I get my desk into my room?" Dickens asked, smirky.

"I have already taken it apart. I will reassemble it inside your space."

"So now his desk or bureau will be two inches from my body when I go to sleep?" Sylvia asked, hoping to prompt some concern.

"This is hickory," her father said, rapping sharply on the wood and then nursing his knuckles. "It will hold up to anything that your brother can do to it or upon it."

"You will be quite safe," Rene said firmly. She was wearing a peacock-green floor-length batik caftan copied from her latest coffee-table purchase, from the used bookstore, about African styles. Sylvia remembered this moment because it was the last time her mother looked as though she was in control of everything, including her father, Sylvia herself and her brother, of planks of wood, and the potential for harm. Two weeks later, Agapito came to tea, disaster in his wake, and the week after, her mother suspended her piano lessons.

As long as Sylvia could remember, her mother had given private piano lessons on her Steinway to children whose fingers she checked at the door, diverting them to the kitchen sink and sometimes applying the nail clippers she had set up on their own silver tray between a bottle of rubbing alcohol and balls of cotton wool in a cut-glass container, for the sole purpose of keeping muck from her most revered possession. Sometimes, Sylvia could tell from the nearly imperceptible flaring and rearrangement of her mother's nostrils, she felt the children themselves were muck, clean fingers and shaped nails notwithstanding. At their best they were a way of distracting herself from her failures, which included the gifted but now only marginally successful husband. It fell to Sylvia to announce to several of them that her mother was not going to be giving lessons for the foreseeable future. It made her feel important but only for as long as it took to utter the words. After that, disappointment gripped her at the thought of losing these ordered but welcome visitations from the outside world. On four occasions, she invited one confused child or another in for a play-lesson that she administered herself. But before long, grappling with the drama of Agapito's arrivals and departures took over Sylvia's life until even she forgot why the occasional young child still rang their doorbell and they had to repeat their hopeful query: *Would Mrs. Rossi be giving piano lessons again?*

Agapito had, until his arrival for tea, communicated with Rene through one of the fifteen female Pew Members who in turn received their wisdom from one of the three male Altar Novices. Rene was an ordinary devotee, and, it turned out, she was the only one without company. Recruitment had hit a low not long after Agapito had made his debut by coming out as a prophet to his yoga class and announcing that he was an incarnation of Christ and would celebrate Christmas on August 29, his own birthday. Rene had joined the class the week after. The others had all preceded her and Rene insisted that she understood her lesser status, but she referred to the hierarchy so often that Sylvia and even Dickens, when Sylvia could get her brother to talk about their mother, felt that this was a singular and deeply painful affront that their mother would remedy before long. And how.

"I have submitted my welcome to Agapito through Crocetta, who is the Pew Member assigned to protect and guide me," Rene said. Then, this: "While he is here, you must refer to me as Ampelio, which means 'vine' in Latin or Greek, I'm not entirely certain, but Crocetta suggested that it would be a good way to draw closer to Agapito. Symbolically."

Sylvia tried it out. "Ampelio, Ampelio, Ampelio. Sounds like a boy's name. How do you know it isn't a boy's name?"

Rene shrugged. "Agapito says that we are sometimes masculine, sometimes feminine."

"So what are you right now?" Dickens asked, scorn etched into his eyebrows. "What am I? Or Syl? Do you have two sons right at this moment or two daughters?"

Her mother did not answer, flat toned or otherwise. In the coming weeks, Sylvia got to know Desiderio and Desideria and Elio, Leonora and Severo and even Ulderico, whom she found particularly winsome and lovely, clad as he was in flowing kurtas, billowing pajamas, and sandals. Agapito himself had been born Paul and had remained so until the Spirit overcame his spirit as he passed the doors of Saint Patrick's Cathedral one summer, his mind still on a woman in a mango-orange dress that he had seen on Fiftieth Street and himself not yet accosted by the panhandler in an equally brilliant red shirt on the corner of Fifty-First Street. Right then, he had stumbled over a piece of plywood left by the workmen realigning the steps to the cathedral and found himself staring at the word *Agapito*, scrawled into wet cement on the pavement alongside a fatly articulated swastika. Sylvia had discovered, during a period of frantic research at her school library, that "Agapito" was derived from "Agapetus," from the Greek αγαπητος or *agapetos*, which meant "beloved," and had, indeed, been the name of two popes.

"Sounds like a pizza," Dickens had said when the story of

Agapito's name was told to them by Rene. "A Greek pizza. With feta."

Perhaps that was why Rene began referring to Agapito as Santo Agapito, which, Dickens told Sylvia, had only simply replaced the Greek ingredients with corn, beans, and cilantro. Sylvia's concerns were more personal: Did she need a new name?

"My name is Zita," she said, bowing low, the first time she was allowed to open the door to him. She held back the long black braids on either side of her face so they wouldn't swing forward and strike Agapito. She had found Zita in a book of baby names and felt moved, she admitted to herself in her journal, by its meaning, which was "little girl," and, she admitted further, its history as the name of the patron saint of servants. Being given to flights of fancy much like her brother, she felt that she served in that role in the house, fetching and carrying all day long.

Agapito, white-on-white-clothed Agapito, standing tall and imposing in the doorway, had looked piercingly into her jade-green eyes with his own that were a shade of watery violet and said nothing for a full count of twelve. That stare had mesmerized Sylvia, and she had felt herself elevated beyond her years. It had been as though he had picked her up and stretched her out and poured secrets into her until she was improved to a stature of womanly grace. But when his eyes moved from her face, she had shrunk down to size, a size that could fit into that house with those parents and the comings and goings of a saint.

Still, Sylvia counted this as her first direct communication with Agapito. It took place when Agapito no longer needed official welcomes to arrive at their doorstep; Rene had been gifted with the designation of Throne Attendant and communicated directly with Agapito himself. Sometimes it wasn't clear which of them was channeling the Spirit to the other. Sometimes, Dickens told Sylvia, he thought that they were so wrapped up in their communication with and transmitting of the Spirit between each other that there was something else going on and it was carnal. Of course, he didn't use those words.

"Do you think they are doing it?" he asked Sylvia one Saturday morning as they lay in what he had declared to be their semi-coffins, though in truth their room was much larger than either of them wanted to concede, it being an easy genesis of solidarity for them, this hardship upon which they could project so many, less tangible, miseries.

"No," Sylvia said. "They can't. We'd hear them through the door."

"Not them, stupid. Agapito and Ampelio."

Sylvia tried to align her right index finger with the pen she could see on her brother's floor through a sliver in the wood above her. "Agapito and Ampelio might," she conceded at last, "but not Paul and Rene. So I don't think they are doing it. Because they aren't really Agapito and Ampelio."

"They might call themselves that just for while they're doing it," her brother suggested.

"Mother wouldn't do that sort of thing," she said. "She's too spiritual."

Her brother scoffed. "Everybody does it."

Sylvia wasn't convinced. It wasn't simply that her mother, wrapped up in her caftans, which had recently given way to lungis and lace jackets picked up from a new coffee-table book with pictures of Thai women, seemed incapable of sex. It was just that she seemed to be a true believer in whatever gospel Agapito was handing out. It was all about achieving the perfect inner balance that would enable her own voice, always a distant second and sometimes third or fourth to her husband's vocal talent, to pour forth.

"Purification is necessary to create a sufficient dwelling for my voice," Rene had said, sitting at the kitchen table. "When that happens, when I have achieved that, my voice will sound with its divine strength. I will reclaim the voice that has eluded me for the last fifteen years."

Sylvia was the only one listening. She was the only one curious about her mother's latest experiment; for she did feel it was an experiment and that it would end as unexpectedly as it had begun, and she wanted to glean the most she could from it while it lasted. "Does Agapito think that your voice has ever been like that?" she asked.

"Like what?"

"The way you said, just now, with the divine strength and all?"

"Speak properly, Sylvia," Rene said and unwrapped a parcel she had brought home along with her Thursday real groceries. Inside a lacquered box was a triangular stringed instrument. Before she could ask, her mother spoke, but softer, so that neither her brother, reading a comic book on the couch, nor her father, practicing "The Street Where You Live" on the very small ledge outside the kitchen, ambitiously named a balcony, could hear had they wanted to listen. "My voice had spirit once before in my life. Before your father. When Sansone met me, I let his voice get inside my body and it buried my own voice. After that, when Dickens was born, and then you, your baby cries shattered my true voice so that now, when I sing, what comes out is only what is available at the top of my body, like when you are holding your breath, not my whole voice. That's what Agapito says."

"That makes sense," Sylvia said, cautiously, not sure if admitting such a thing meant she was forgiven for having splintered her mother's voice, but feeling that whatever part of the blame could be assigned to her, it had to be minimal, since much of the sundering had gone on before she was born.

"It does. It does." Rene nodded as she plucked at the strings of the instrument in front of her.

"What is that for?"

"This is for Agapito to help coax out whatever he can of the pieces of my voice."

"But it won't be in pieces when you are clean. Cleansed, I mean. Right?" Sylvia asked.

"Yes, but cleansing will take a very long time. These strings, when plucked right, will waken those parts of my voice that are lost and help them to find each other. That way, when the final cleansing is done, they will be able to surge forth, upward, up, up, through my body and throat and out!" As she spoke, Rene rose to her feet and then to her toes, finishing with uplifted face and hands outstretched over her head.

Sylvia, gazing up at her mother, didn't think the lungi and lace blouse worked with this spectacle. "I think the caftan suited you better," she volunteered, yearning now to be part of the solution. "I think it was more like your voice is going to be. Flowing."

Rene returned to the full length of her soles and stared at Sylvia. She leaned forward and gripped her shoulders. "You understand. Sylvia! You understand! You are right. The caftans must come back!"

"The caftans must come back!" Sylvia echoed. She jumped to her feet and hugged her mother, basking in this rare moment of lightness.

But the caftans only came back for a week. Agapito dismissed them as inappropriate, which had the effect of Sylvia being looked upon with some self-conscious scorn by her own mother for a while and, most especially, when she bowed low and said "Welcome, Santo Agapito, I am Zita," by Agapito himself, who turned away from her as if to avoid being tainted by the spouting of a charlatan. Not long after, her mother took up the peasant dresses of her youth.

"I think it is because it reminds her of what it was like to be her before she met Papa," Sylvia told Dickens, letting her voice find him through the cracks of her ceiling, his floor.

"Why would she want to remember that time? She used to be nobody until she met him," Dickens said, returning the favor with his uncharged voice, making her work to hear him.

"She's nobody now," Sylvia said, which was true, at least by her mother's assessment.

—

Rene had a history of enthusiasms she had claimed would elevate her from obscurity to fame, but unlike all the other attempts Rene had made to change the direction of her life, Agapito was not fading. Agapito was rising; he was rising in influence, and presence in their lives. Sylvia began to worry. When she came home from school now, instead of seeking the refuge of her half of the Swastika, still available to her when the full meeting was not in session, she spent time in the kitchen. With whatever unpredictable noise she could make by clattering tea kettles and whooshing fridge doors and even the furious application of serrated knives to loaves of bread, she tried to snip the connection between her mother and Agapito, which she pictured as a silver cord undulating between their foreheads like she had observed happened in movies that featured aliens; aliens always communicated with zigzag bolts of lightning. At this hour, Agapito and Rene sat face-to-face, cross-legged before the brightest window in the living room, and the cord was almost tangible. This was the time of day when, Agapito had decided, the house was least occupied by the sounds that had been uttered by Sansone and the children. For a full hour, Agapito tugged at a string on the triangle, and her mother would hum the note. She often got it wrong, which prompted Sylvia to hum it softly and correctly in the kitchen, willing her mother to get it right and make Agapito redundant. It did not happen.

And Sansone? Her father was busy. He, like Dickens, wasted no mind on Ampelio and Agapito. He had no time for Paul either. He dealt only with Rene, and only if she left her spirituality out of their conversation. Sometimes, he even played the Steinway—that surely had to have been lofted onto their floor before the apartment walls had been constructed around it—and he listened to Rene sing, offering suggestions and making small alterations in pitch and tone. A few times he invited her out on the balcony when he practiced. These occasions had been so infrequent in the past that Sylvia experienced them as being unspeakably fragile indications of harmony that she had to encourage by becoming completely still, hardly breathing. Now she found it disturbing, this intimacy, as two worlds nudged at and ignored each other. How could her papa and mother coexist with grace when Agapito and Ampelio conducted themselves with such proximate intensity about matters of life and soul and, worse, the reconstitution of a voice that was deemed to be lying in smithereens inside her voluptuous body? How could her papa compare? No, Sylvia felt, an end had better come and the quicker the better.

"Don't you wish we had our room back?" she asked Dickens one morning.

"They use it mostly when we're not here anyway," Dickens said.

"But it's our room. Why can't they meet somewhere else?" Sylvia poked her toe through a small hole that had appeared in one plank of wood and that she had worked at with her foot until it became large enough to insert a part of herself in this way into her brother's space.

"I don't care," her brother replied. "You shouldn't either. She won't be doing this for much longer."

"How do you know? It feels like it will never end," Sylvia said, trying not to sound as though she was whining. She would turn twelve soon and should really be spending more time on accumulating her own regrets and strange behaviors, not being so preoccupied with rescuing her mother from hers. Even if this latest disruption had dragged on for a full year and six weeks from the time her mother signed up for the yoga class. Seven months to the day from Agapito's first visit to their house. Three months and a few days since the weekly meeting had moved into their bedroom.

Sylvia had only witnessed the meeting once and not because she was invited but by climbing out onto the balcony, standing on the curving wrought iron balustrade, and craning her neck first over Dickens's half and then under the lip of her half of the one window to their room. What she saw was this: Agapito seated rather comfortably on a fat jeweled cushion on her brother's bed, while her mother knelt before him. Four other women, all facing outward in each of the four directions, held hands and squeezed back to back on her floor. They all had long hair and similar body types, generous in all regards. That was the root of Sylvia's suspicion: she distrusted men who surrounded themselves with women who looked like they should be in European paintings; suckling infants or spread in an overly lavish manner on curved furniture or dangling themselves from trees, creamy flesh protruding from their garments in a seemingly natural manner, as if they had been surprised in the nude by their artist friends. Adding to this discomfort, for Sylvia, was the fact that the structural integrity of the Swastika was being severely compromised by the adult bodies within it. The window was shut, so all Sylvia heard was what she guessed by lip-reading the impassioned members of the flock on the floor: "Come, come, come, come, come, now!" which was repeated three times and ended with everybody flinging their heads forward to the floor (or bed or chair) and back so far their unfocused eyes rolled in their heads. After a few minutes of this, she had struggled down from her perch and returned to the kitchen to eat a roast-beef sandwich with mayonnaise from her father's stash in the mini refrigerator to which Rene had consigned her husband's "contaminants."

"I wish they would stop it," Sylvia said now to her brother, feeling petulant.

"Everything ends with Mother, you know that. This one will too. It's just taking a little longer because of the whole god thing."

"They don't have a real god," Sylvia said. "If they did have one, then Mother might have given up a while ago. She always expects gods to do things quickly. This time it's about something coming from Agapito and something found inside her own self. That doesn't have a time limit. She said so herself."

Dickens groaned, a long guttural softened by his pillow. "I don't want to go to school."

"Let's not, then," Sylvia said. "Let's stay here and spy on them."

"That's boring."

Sylvia sighed. If she couldn't think of something that would interest Dickens, they would just end up going to school. "Agapito is allergic to nuts," she said, though this was mere hope, not certainty. Lately there had been a spate of fresh allergies announced at school and the lowly peanut seemed to be sweeping the nation as a secret killer.

"So?"

"So we could put peanuts in our room and then he won't come here anymore."

There was silence and then Dickens giggled; she hadn't heard that sound in a long time and it made her smile. Her brother had been fun before he turned thirteen and got smart. "We don't have peanuts in the house," he said.

"But we can get them from somewhere."

So they got dressed and went to school, and on the way back, they bought peanuts. And even though it took a full one-eighth of their combined allowances to buy raw peanuts, which, Dickens said, would probably be worse for Agapito than those that had been roasted, it felt worth it to Sylvia. It took them a good hour to hide the peanuts in all the cracks in the boards that made up their S for Swastika room. Sylvia felt a particularly acute sense of virtue when she blocked up the toe hole that she had worked so hard to create. Dickens, for his part, sacrificed the long crack alongside his bed that he had been using to throw trash into Sylvia's space. They brushed their teeth and went to bed, and Sylvia whispered a heartfelt goodnight to Dickens, assured of Agapito's mysterious eviction from their bedroom and, hopefully, as the negative association with the apartment took root, a permanent departure from her mother's life as well.

Agapito did not succumb, a fact Sylvia explained to Dickens as being on account of his sainthood, and which explanation finally validated Agapito's claim to being one in Dickens's eyes, even if only slightly. Agapito continued to hold meetings in their room long past her own birthday—which was not celebrated—before he fell ill, and came to live or, rather, die in their company.

"He will be with us until the end," their mother said, and installed Agapito on the floor of their living room, where he reclined on a bed inflated, rather irreligiously, Sylvia felt, with a foot pump. What ailed him was unclear. The only visible change was that he moved more slowly than he had done before, which meant he hardly moved at all. When he raised his limbs in the contemplative manner that was his trademark, to accept a glass of water perhaps or to bless a bowed head, the movement seemed to cause him pain. Not that he complained; he was, Rene had told her children, above such mortal preoccupations as pain and sickness. Sylvia just knew it because of the length of time it took him to accomplish these small things and mostly because of the way his devotees furrowed their brows with concern, their own bodies tilting forward as if to offer themselves up as surrogate limbs and torsos.

And Sansone? Her father continued to come home for meals, talk to her mother, shower, and even practice his singing on the balcony, an act which, Sylvia could see quite plainly, compounded

Agapito's discomfort, but he slept elsewhere. Her mother did not tell them where. When he was around, he referred to the devotees with a certain affectionate tolerance as the Butterballs, took obvious pride in his prior claim to their sacred space and their high priestess, and always offered to make an extra sandwich in case they were hungry. Nobody took him up on his offers and nobody spoke to him directly.

—

"I will need the two of you to move out of your bedroom for the passing," Rene said one Saturday morning, coming in to their bedroom while traces of their conversation about the goings-on outside and the money misspent on raw peanuts still hung in the air.

"Passing of what?" Dickens asked from his perch at Sylvia's desk. His voice sounded bored, a clear effort, Sylvia knew, to distract her mother from sensing the irreverent leftovers from their previous conversation.

"Is it Passover?" Sylvia asked, sitting up. "My friend Rachel says that's the Jewish spring holiday, but they eat special bread and drink wine." In truth, Rachel wasn't Sylvia's friend. In truth, Sylvia had no friends but her brother. Still, she felt an overheard conversation could be taken to have been a participatory one if some part of her was touching some part of the group, even her shadow. Usually it was her shadow. She rarely participated during the noon hours, when even her shadow left her alone.

"This is not the time to make light of our circumstances," Rene said, having taken a few moments to look toward the floor, gather herself, and raise her head to face them again. "Santo Agapito is dying."

Was that a catch in her mother's throat? It had to be, of course, it would make sense, but her mother, though given to bouts of hysterical rage, was not given to expressions of grief. Grief was considered a capitulation whereas rage was positive and directional. Rene's ground rule for the conduct of her life was stoicism in the face of adversity, anything less being construed to indicate a lack of breeding. Breeding had always been important to Rene, though whether she had acquired it herself or only aspired to do so was still unclear to Sylvia.

"Is he going to die today?" Sylvia asked, with a hint of cheerfulness she failed to conceal. She moved to a side to make room for her brother, who had climbed down to join her.

"Sylvia, I do not know when he will pass from us. Santo Agapito has only let us know that he will be leaving us."

"What happens to the . . . the meeting, then?" Sylvia asked, her tongue almost betraying her with the word *cult*.

"Santo Agapito will not be leaving us forever. He will rise again."

Sylvia gazed at her mother. Rene leaned against the doorpost. She was dressed in a white peasant dress and had taken to tying strands of beaded strings around her forehead. The two did not go together. Her mother looked mad. Crazy mad. The only normal thing about her was her speech. "I need you, Dickens, to take charge of moving your belongings out of this room," Rene said.

"But where are we going to move to? This is where we live!" Dickens said, his palms outstretched. He flopped down on the bed next to Sylvia.

"You will move into the living room. Agapito must lie here."

"What about Papa?"

"I have asked your father to stay away until the passing and resurrection," Rene said. Sylvia would have liked to ask more questions: dates, times, planned activities, rituals. She would have liked to know if her father had agreed to this altered sleeping arrangement with equanimity or whether he had fought. When had the discussion taken place? Who had initiated it? If he had argued, for whom had he spoken, for himself or for them? Most importantly, was her mother going to be the chief caregiver of Agapito's decaying body? What if he did not rise? Would he have to stay forever? But these were not the words to utter in the face of prescience, so she began stacking her books and clothes on her bed.

"What does he have?" Dickens asked their mother, startling Sylvia, who had, just at that moment, seen a stray peanut on the floor close to her mother's foot.

"He doesn't have any known disease. He is willingly giving up his body so we can return him to life cleansed of the brutalities he has endured in the past."

Sylvia sighed with relief. "That's good," she said, forgetting herself.

"I don't understand. He's just deciding to die?" Dickens asked. "Isn't that considered suicide? Is he committing suicide? Isn't that illegal? Are we accessories after the fact?" He had recently begun to read Perry Mason detective novels and had also introduced them to Sylvia, who seconded his inquiry with a murmur.

Rene simply stared at her son and said nothing. After a long while she heaved off the door frame, came completely into their room, and touched each of their heads. It was like a whisper above their heads, that hand, barely grazing the top layers of hair. Then she fell to her knees and clutched them both fiercely to her. That was a shock and Sylvia looked in some consternation at her brother over her mother's head. His arms were, like hers, pinned to his sides, and his eyes bulged comically, but he didn't try to wriggle out of the embrace. Just as abruptly, Rene let them go, stood up, told them she would be back shortly—the whole congregation was assembling at Crocetta's to discuss the rituals for that evening and the ensuing days, as long as it was necessary—and left the room. A few moments later they heard the front door close.

"Why did Papa leave without telling us?" Sylvia asked her

brother, not expecting a reply. She listened to him gathering his stuff above her head.

"He's never told us where he's going before, and he always comes back later," Dickens said. He poked his head through the stairs to his floor and watched her for a few minutes.

"I don't think you have to be that neat about packing, Syl. We're just moving these things into the living room. We're not moving house."

"I hate Agapito. I hope he dies soon," Sylvia said.

"Darn!" Dickens exclaimed after a brief silence. "We better get the peanuts out of here!" He climbed down the rest of the way.

"Why? He's already dying. Why would it matter?"

"I don't want them to find out. Mother would be furious. And the whole point was for him to get sick and go away, which isn't going to happen now. He's chosen to kill himself inside our— this—our box!"

"I don't want to do any more than I have to."

"I'm getting rid of them. They didn't work, and I don't want any further trouble."

Sylvia flopped onto her back in her bed and watched her brother pry at the peanuts that sealed the hole in his floor. They fell with a small rustle onto her feet. She entertained the idea of kicking them off but resisted. If Dickens had decided, then the peanuts would have to go one way or another. She collected them into a single pile and started to eat them.

"Come on, Sylvia, I don't want to be doing everything by myself and we still have to move all our stuff."

"Fine, I'll help," Sylvia said. She got a dustpan and began sweeping up the nuts that kept falling from above along the side of her brother's bed, down his stairs, off the windowsill. It sounded like benevolent, albeit uncertain, hail.

At the far end of the corridor that separated their bedrooms from the living room, basket in hand, she stopped at the sound of a new noise: Agapito had begun to moan very softly. She put the basket down and walked over to the bed on which he lay, propped on king-sized pillows covered in silk pillowcases that didn't match; one was lime green and the other was yellow. On the very white linen sheets that Rene washed by hand, dried, and ironed every two days, the pillows looked very bright. His eyes were closed. Agapito in this state was not as enigmatic as he had previously seemed to be to Sylvia. His face, once the angular evidence of deprivation underpinned by moral fortitude, was now simply a long face; his body, an ordinary thinness exacerbated by bones that had overreached to a few inches above six feet. Even his hair, long though it was, and silken, Sylvia knew, from contriving to caress it accidentally in passing during better times, when she had still assumed him to be a glamorous transient, was no grander than the locks of any of the women she'd met at the theaters where her papa performed.

"Are you going to die today?" Sylvia whispered, after staring at Agapito's face for a few moments. "Not that I want you to die or anything. I just wondered if you knew."

"Butter," Agapito murmured. "Butter." He said the word with great effort, which seemed to proclaim both longing and irritation.

"It's the butter that's made you ill," Sylvia said. "My brother and I agree. My papa would, too, if he were here. I can make you a sandwich. We have roast beef . . ."

Agapito moaned again. His right forearm flopped a few times and then settled, passing the activity to his wrist and fingers, which twitched unhappily and gave up.

"Do you happen to know when you might rise?" Sylvia persisted, feeling irritated. How bad could his pain be if he knew he was just going to come back all fresh and healthy? It seemed ungenerous of him to make so much of it at this point, given that the rest of his flock had only one life to live.

"Sylvia! Why aren't you helping? We're supposed to be done before Mother gets back!"

Sylvia turned to face her brother, who had come out of their room laden with books. "What if we catch what he's got by sleeping where he's slept?" she asked.

"Just get your stuff out," Dickens said. He began to walk away but turned around to face her as another moan escaped from Agapito's cracked lips. "Is he talking to you?" he asked.

"No, he's just asking for butter."

Dickens came up to her and stared at Agapito. "He's dying, Sylvia. This might be his last wish. Give him some butter."

"You give him butter. I'm not touching him."

Her brother stacked his books under the piano and went into the kitchen and returned carrying a pot of clarified butter made by Rene and a long silver spoon. The change from plain butter to clarified butter had been in response to Agapito's illness and the pot was so recently made that it smelled like freshly popped corn.

"Make sure he doesn't cough or spit on you. Germs," Sylvia cautioned as her brother knelt beside Agapito.

"Santo Agapito, the butter is here," Dickens said in what Sylvia felt was a voice too imbued with reverence, given that he had never liked Agapito, let alone made any inquiries as to the source of his convictions the way she herself had done, and given that he shared her deep desire to see him dead, risen, and departed as soon as was humanly possible.

Agapito moaned. Dickens took the opportunity to slide a spoonful of butter between Agapito's lips. Agapito spat. He made a guttural sound that was very loud, even angry.

"He must know you don't have a real name," Sylvia said, "like mine, like Zita."

"I'm Dickens!" her brother said, with some consternation, to Agapito. "I'm Mother's—I mean Rene's, I mean Ampelio's—son!"

He dipped the spoon back into the butter as he talked and scooped up a fresh golden offering.

"Now you've gone and contaminated the clarified butter," Sylvia said. "Now all his germs are in the butter."

They argued about the butter for a few moments, their words punctuated by more moaning and further requests for butter from Agapito, which did not appear to be well thought out because he spat each time Dickens tried to feed him. It did not occur to either of them that Agapito was gone, that it was Paul who was lying there, that he was asking for water, not butter, and that he did not want to die.

"Look, he's crying," Dickens said. Sure enough, slow-moving tears tipped the corners of Agapito's eyes.

"I hope Mother comes back soon with the others," Sylvia said, realizing for the first time that Agapito might actually perish before their eyes. "We don't know any death rites and we can't move him!"

"Quick. Let's empty our bedroom so they can get him in there as soon as they come back," Dickens said.

Together they scurried in and out of their room, shoving their belongings as far back as they would go under the closed Steinway and, when that was crammed, stacking their bedding on top of the orange couch. When they were done, Dickens swept their room.

"Now it really looks like a jail again," he said.

"Should we check on him?" Sylvia asked.

She slowed her steps as they neared the mattress. Sylvia noticed that the pot of butter had been knocked over. Agapito's foot lay suspiciously close to it.

"I don't think he's dead yet. See? I think he kicked it."

"Should we clean it?" Dickens asked, which meant he didn't want to but felt that she should.

"I'll clean it." Sylvia mopped the floor with wet paper towels and a sponge as Dickens watched. "Mother will be furious. It's so hard to make."

"Papa says that's just something called ghee and you can buy it at Indian grocery stores."

"Papa should be here looking after us," Sylvia said, her eyes welling up as she contemplated having to face both a dead body and her mother without anyone to protect them.

"Don't cry," Dickens said. "Look, he's still moaning, so he's alive. It doesn't look like he'll die before Mother gets back."

They sat cross-legged a few feet away and listened to his wheezing, gurgling requests for butter, which they no longer honored; they strained forward when he grew quiet and looked like he had fallen asleep; they jumped with alarm each time he started up again. Then, after a particularly long bout, he stopped breathing.

"Should we call someone? A neighbor?" Sylvia asked.

"Let's wait," Dickens said.

"But he's dead."

"Only for a short time. He's going to rise again." Dickens didn't sound convincing.

A terrifying doubt unfurled around Sylvia. "They're not here to raise him!"

"Don't scream!" Dickens yelled.

Agapito murmured beside them.

"He's risen!" Sylvia said, her voice a tearful squeal of joy. She hugged her equally delighted brother, exclaiming over their good fortune at being present for the miracle of resurrection, if not able to claim that their devotion had caused it to be. She was still laughing when her mother returned.

"Mother! Agapito died and then came back to life! It's already happened. The miracle. We saw it. We were here. Dickens and I, we saw it!" Sylvia was ecstatic, her euphoria added to by the knowledge that:

1. Agapito would leave,
2. her mother had finally been right to believe something, and
3. she, Sylvia, had played a small role in the events.

She decided to have Zita tagged onto her name as a silent initial. When she was grown up, she could dispense with her last name and be no more, no less than the sum of her experiences: Sylvia Z.

"What?" The question escaped in a breath through her open lips in a way that made Sylvia anxious. Perhaps her mother was angry that she had missed the whole affair. Perhaps details, and the fact of how recent the death and revival had been, might make her mother feel more a part of it?

"We looked after him! We made sure he had everything he wanted. First he wanted butter and then he spat it out and he kicked it away and we cleaned that up, and then, because it seemed as though he was beginning to die, we cleaned our whole room." Her mother hardly seemed to be listening. Sylvia reached out, took her hand, and led her to their empty room. "Look!" she said, waving her arm with as much of a sweep as was permitted, and merited, by the cramped space. "It was waiting to receive his body but it's not needed anymore."

"Sylvia, let go of me," her mother said, her voice trembling.

"Santo Agapito has returned," Sylvia continued, desperate, "just like you said he would. Now he can . . . now he can . . ." But she couldn't finish her sentence, for how could she communicate her desire to be rid of the man when her mother appeared to be so stricken? Rene was clattering back to Agapito in her clogs, having forgotten to remove them at the door, a custom established by rules of cleanliness laid even before the advent of Agapito and the accompanying lists of dos and don'ts.

"Agapito! Santo Agapito!" her mother wailed, on her knees, her palms around his left hand, her head bowing repeatedly onto his narrow chest. Agapito moaned, but it was not a specific communication, one directed at his cherished Ampelio, but rather a generic utterance whose source appeared to be some all-too-mortal discomfort or, even more shockingly, regret, being experienced right then by him.

The sound of her mother crying, and the clear evidence that it had not been a distaste of sorrow that had kept her from outward expression of that emotion but rather the absence of anything worthwhile to call it forth, including all of the difficulties she and her brother had experienced over the years, caused a sharp misalignment to inhabit Sylvia's body. She walked unsteadily over to her brother, who was still standing watch over Agapito. "If he's better, why hasn't he got up?" she asked him.

Dickens shrugged. "I don't know."

Fear gripped Sylvia around her chest. Had they, in their unintentional resurrection of Agapito, brought about, she was sure, by their deep and combined misery at having to cope with a dead body rather than a steadfast belief in his doctrine, let alone his plans for their mother, caused a malfunction in the order of events? Had they doomed their mother's saint to eternal death by their interference?

"He . . . Agapa . . . Aga . . . Santo Agapito might want more butter," she offered to her mother's curved and grieving spine. "That might help," she added when her mother did not respond.

"Go!" her mother said, but it was more of a low moan, trapped somewhere between her chin and neck. It was not comforting. It did not bespeak a found voice.

"Shall we call Papa?" Dickens asked, after casting a sympathetic glance at Sylvia.

"Go!" her mother said again, more of a growl.

"If he's not yet dead," Sylvia volunteered, feeling things spiraling out of control and, through long experience, fearing the outcome, "then we can help you put him in the Swastika Room!"

And this time there was no recognizable word to go with the snarl that broke free from Rene's body. It was a sound deep and pure and so full of strength that it hit Sylvia full in her stomach. It flung her to the couch, where she scrambled onto the bedding they had stacked on it, slipping as she went up onto the cushions behind it and back from there to the ledge of their living room window to the thick purple drapes that she wrapped around herself, tighter and tighter until they gave way under her weight and she fell in a clumsy heap to an area behind the couch where she stayed, balled into the heavy purple fabric like a seed inside a giant grape, sobbing.

And for what did she mourn? For her papa, who was not six feet and was portly but had a voice so beautiful that if he were with them, this other sound would never have burst forth from her mother but would have stayed in its thousand benign severed pieces. For her papa, who was so weak that he would allow a demon to enter his household and rename his wife and frighten his children and turn them out of their own bedroom. For her papa, who slept on a fold-out couch and sang small songs on a window ledge and made coffins with his own hands for his living daughter and son.

Sylvia refused to come out of her purple sack or to speak for three days, except when taken by her hand and led, her eyes shut, to the bathroom or the sink by her brother, who faithfully returned her to her chosen place of refuge. On the third day, Dickens, who had been bringing her food from their father's refrigerator, and news of the world outside, joined her.

"They have laid him on your floor," he had told her on the first day. "He died again, this time for good, I think."

"They are praying over his body," he told her on the second day.

"They lit candles. They're holding hands and they take turns dripping butter on his forehead, chest, and feet."

"Some of them have left," he told her on the morning of the third day. And in the afternoon, "It doesn't smell very good there." By evening he had crept under the drapes with her, where, he told her, though she had just wet herself, it didn't smell as bad.

And Sansone? By the time he returned, nearly two weeks after he had left, the house had been emptied of its guests, including the body of Agapito, which had been carried out under the cover of darkness, wrapped in the white linen sheets and propped inside the dumbwaiter, to Crocetta's flat at 60 Riverside Drive, on Seventy-Eighth Street, after the neighbors complained of a stench. The swastika had been removed, piece by piece, by his wife. There she sat, at the kitchen table, looking at her bruised hands in silence. She refused to acknowledge him and left to join the wake as soon as he had taken off his shoes, hat, and jacket. He found his children behind the couch. They would not tell him what had happened, or why they were hiding. They only folded into his sweaty, unfulfilled body and stayed there.

And even though her father crawled into the space behind the couch with them and told them stories about the theater, the way he had always reclaimed their affections after being gone, Sylvia knew that his meek presence would never again be worth what it had once been to her. To ease her heart of the pain this knowledge brought her, she asked him to sing.

"An old song, Papa," she said, "something we have never heard before." She waited a long time for him to begin and was startled when he did. His voice was unlike all the others she had heard him use to give wings to his songs, playing the roles that he went out seeking and came home regretting. It was a short song that he sang, and he repeated it, again and again, until both she and Dickens fell asleep. Sylvia did not see, nor would it have mattered if she had, that her father was weeping. The rest of her life had already begun.

Beauty Treatments

The moment that Suzanne, no-last-name, the Grand Dame of Venus Day Spa & Bistro, laid her salve-softened seventy-seven-year-old hands on her feet, Maya cringed. Her feet, accustomed to being bare unless absolutely necessary, were never going to respond to the kind of ministrations such hands could provide. This was followed by irritation: Why did Suzanne have to touch her feet in the first place? She had signed up for a spa facial, not a foot massage.

"This will create the right relaxation, my dear, before we begin to work on your face," Suzanne said, reading her mind. Of course.

Suzanne's voice was deep, but not in the way cigarettes deepened voices. This was a spiritual deepening. She had probably been born with a happy American voice until the discovery of yoga and meditation and ingredients with names like babassu and carnauba and murumuru butter—Maya had read them off the labels on the pots and potions in the waiting room—had probably hastened her ascension to the kind of Awareness that eluded Maya, the kind of inward focus that had led to the corresponding descent to the pitch of her voice.

Maya sighed.

"Relax, dear," Suzanne said, her palms barely touching Maya's ankles, soles, and each of her ten toes.

Maya concentrated on relaxing. Within a surprisingly short time, her feet, which she had been holding steadfastly together, separated and fell willingly and comfortably apart onto the soft, rolled towel beneath them.

Still, that was just the feet. She wouldn't have to apologize for her feet. She would make sure that she cleaned them up before she came for round two of her treatment. But what would she do about her face? Her face would betray her, this much was certain. That made her feel bad. She felt bad in advance of whatever care Suzanne had in store for her and it was quite clear that if Suzanne had anything, it was a bottomless store of care.

It wasn't that she, Maya, was timid, no. In fact, she was an inveterate fixer. The kind who had a feasible solution, clearly delineated and publicly stated and not without a certain and often overpowering vehemence. If there was a problem, she leaped to find solutions. Particularly for her family, but also for her friends and, in numerous columns appearing in local papers and online forums, for larger issues: the Palestinians, the Iraqis, Beirut, Benazir Bhutto, Bombay. These were reasons to be moved and moved she had been. So, no, she was not timid. But there was an oddly compulsive concern for the history of individual human beings, for lives lived, the "sorries," as she liked to put it, privately, that filled her with disquiet. Which is why, today, as she lay supine on the raised bed, the overtones of quasi-Ayurvedic greens about her, New Age music rising and falling somewhere off center, the lights dimmed and the air heavy with the perfume of well-being, she was wracked with guilt.

Two facts. One: Maya had bad skin. Two: Suzanne was determined to fix it. Well, four facts: Maya brought tropical brown skin to the table and Suzanne's remedies were cooked up in laboratories. In other words, the twain would meet but the peace process was doomed.

"Didn't you say your mother was visiting?" Suzanne murmured, inverted over her face, eyes to lips, nose to nose, and smoothed a pale lilac-colored salve over her face that instantly cooled her skin.

"Yes, she's here."

"You must be happy to see her," Suzanne stated the assumed fact. Into the silence that followed she launched a different question. "How is she liking this cold weather?"

"It's been difficult with her here," Maya said. Was it because this was something she could offer Suzanne, who would find no refuge in her stubborn skin? Or was it the combination of substances, sounds, affects soaking into her body through her willing pores, those parted feet? "She is very unhappy and all she wants to talk about is the past and I feel that I'm trying to escape that, forget about it, the past, and just trying to move on with my life. Be happy."

Underneath her masses of jet-black hair, now being massaged, inexplicably, by Suzanne, Maya cursed at herself. How utterly American to make such revelations; with what ease she had unlocked the door and pushed those demons out like so many bad children being sent abroad for fresh air.

"I had a mother like that," Suzanne said. She came around to the right side of Maya's body and linked her fingers through Maya's in what Maya at first assumed was a show of solidarity but then discovered was simply a continuation of the massage for which, again, she had not signed up but that she was now finding decidedly comforting. "My mother left me when she went off to work because she wanted fine things. A lot of fine things. I was left alone."

Suzanne's face was old, but her skin was taut and clear, almost supple. She had bird marks around her eyes, and her lipstick made tracery paths away from her mouth as though each set were emissaries. Still, she was clearly healthy. She kept a juicer in the salon and drank elixirs concocted of organic kale, beet greens, lettuce, carrots, and apples, she told Maya. Her eight daughters and one son, who all worked at the salon or were in the process of fleeing or returning to it, thought it looked unappetizing, she continued, as she discussed the importance of nutrition in skin care, but she persisted. Maya had commended her on her discipline and remarked about the quality of Suzanne's skin; both compliments were, clearly, welcome but not needed by the older woman to confirm her good sense and disposition toward the management of her inner health and outer appearance. Maya looked at Suzanne full in the face for the first time now, caught between three conflicting emotions: her enjoyment of the kneading of her right hand, arm, and shoulder; the sensation that the left side of her body was cold and neglected; and her relief that Suzanne had actually heard what she had said. Her embarrassment over her strange outburst evaporated into the room.

"Where is she now?" Maya asked, a little less tentative.

"She died eleven years ago. I looked after her till she died, but it was very hard for me. I resented having to do it. I couldn't tell her."

"I wish I could tell my mother various things, things about the past, what happened to me, but I can't. I spend so much time thinking about how to tell her and so most of the day I don't talk to her at all. She thinks I'm not talking to her, but I am. Just in my head."

"It was the same with me. I finally wrote her a letter," Suzanne said.

"That's a possibility, I suppose. If I could bring myself to put it down in black and white."

Suzanne went on with her own confidences. "I wrote her a letter and told her. You know what her response was? *What do you expect me to do about it?*" She blinked several times as she said that. She was still massaging Maya's right arm. Despite the gravity of their respective almost disclosures, Maya couldn't help wondering if Suzanne would forget her left side altogether or, if she did remember, if their conversation would by then still be serious enough to merit the same amount of time and intensity.

"Can you imagine? From a mother? You know, I've raised my children differently. I always stayed home. We didn't have much, my husband and I, but I always cooked at home, and the children have grown up close to us. None of them want to be far away from the family. They're all here with me. My daughter, the one who left for a little while to live in Portland, even she came back."

Maya found an opening. "Maine's a good place for a family," she said. "Waterville, I mean. It's a small town, and even though it doesn't have lots of things, it's got enough. What I find about cities is that there is so much of everything, yet the people who live there, even us, when we lived in the city, we didn't go to any of those things. The restaurants, we couldn't afford them. Here we have just that place, the Riverside Farm Market, and their food is delicious . . ." Maya trailed away, her thoughts on the low wood building sitting on the crest of a hill over the Kennebec River, which wound itself between the pines like a misplaced reflective silk scarf. There she sat now, enjoying the air and, before her on the table, a grilled salmon sandwich with organic spinach, roasted red peppers, and mozzarella on a crusty home-baked roll. What might she have afterward?

Suzanne, standing beside Maya's bliss-resistant body, broke into this reverie with a fresh slap of warm oil and her story. "My children came back to me. I didn't have that kind of feeling about my mother. I never wanted to go back. I finally decided that I needed to separate myself from that past. I looked after her until she died, because she had nowhere else to go, but that was it. My husband was good to me; if you have a good husband, then everything is different. He worked, I stayed home. Then, when the children were older, I started the salon. They all work here now. My children all work here now."

"I know," Maya said. "They seem nice."

"They wanted to be with us. They wanted to be with me. They came back. Except the one, but even she came back."

"That's extremely fortunate," Maya said. "Very few families stay close like that."

"You have to let it go."

"Yes, I know," Maya said.

"You just have to let it go. That past, it's not you. It's what happened and you just do what you must to leave it behind."

Maya made a sound of assent, a sound like *hmm*, a contemplative concurrence on Suzanne's all-American prescription for life. She wanted to suspect the potency of Suzanne's balms and potions, for how could those be any more specific to her particular conditions than these kinds of platitudes? But Suzanne moved over to the other side and picked up Maya's left arm and Maya was distracted. Her right now felt welded to the table in a contented torpor. She swiveled her head so she could see Suzanne's face again; the dried herbs and grain inside the pillow rustled and released a stronger scent. It was like having a conversation with dead plants and taped music, almost eerie except that it was so intensely gratifying. Suzanne's eyes remained on the limb she held, and there was no more conversation. After a length of time, neither too long nor too short, so that Maya could not claim that she felt unbalanced on either side of her body, Suzanne wiped her hands on the sheet under Maya. She spent the next several minutes wiping off the lilac salve she had used with warm pads of gauze, then applied a European mud masque to her face and neck. Maya opened her eyes. Suzanne patted her arm, then drifted out of sight behind her head and returned, briefly, into her line of sight before disappearing again behind the cool, fragrant pads that were placed over Maya's eyes.

"How do you feel? Are you warm enough?" she asked.

Maya nodded.

"I'm going to leave you here for a while so that the mud has time to work, and then I'll be back. Stay quiet, dear."

It wasn't as though she was going to rise off the bed, this seeming cloud of luxury upon which she had willingly cast herself and where she had received more than she had paid for or expected. *Stay quiet*, she repeated to herself, silently in her head, then whispered into the room. "Stay quiet, stay quiet, stay quiet." They were well-balanced words, those two. A good beginning, the important combination of full and half vowels between, and the near repeat of the ending consonant. Together, they were up-and-down words, the way a child would use a paintbrush to test colors on a piece of white paper, or draw water, mostly blue.

Blue water surrounded her island home, though the rivers mostly ran gray and taupe with silt churned up by monsoon rains. Except when it flooded and then the water was caramel and she would imagine that they were depositing precious stones among the hovels that lined the banks. Yes, it had been important to imagine that, curdled into the thick cow-dung walls disintegrating under the silently rising water, there were uncut star rubies, peacock-blue sapphires, creamy cat's-eyes, garnets. Hopeful things, a way out of misery for anybody who wished to look.

And she had looked, hadn't she? Every time she came home from school, she had dug in the sands. Dug and dug while her feet sank slowly into the muddied slope outside her home, dug until her arms were elbow high in sludge, until she forgot what she was digging for and began to shape bowls and plates out of the earth, imagining that if she made enough, she could sell them outside the temple gates. Sell them and collect shiny silver coins to put into her clay till, which was shaped like an elephant, which she loved and which she would have to break when it was full, feeling the longing and the dread at the same time.

"My mother left me," she said, aloud, although she was now alone. "She went to work as a housemaid for two years and when she came back, we had enough money to move away from the river-bank. We moved to a real house with water bills and electricity bills and my sisters and I had to study even harder so we wouldn't have to go back to our hut. We would only go farther from the river, from the possibility of precious discoveries. My husband came to our house as a boarder. He was studying rural sociology in Boston and I became his translator and then his wife. That's how."

She stopped. She didn't know what more she could add to this tale, and having released it into the sweetly unctuous room, she wanted to take it all back. She lay there and pictured the story re-winding as she sucked the words into her mouth, back to her brain, and from there to silence: ".how That's. wife his then and translator his became I and Boston in sociology rural studying was He." She couldn't remember the precise sentences she had used before that one, so she switched to pictures: a young American arriving at their house in khaki pants and cotton shirt and backpack on his back; she and her sister studying, staying up late, waking up early, being first in their respective classes, first in everything; moving to the new house with its three rooms, one for the family to sleep in, one for the cheap sitting room furniture her mother had bought, one for cooking and eating; the path to the new house as it was constructed, brick by brick; the road on the rise above the old hut; not first in everything; the hut itself, so worn and smooth and made fresh from scratch after each flood; the earth; the unfound jewels; the rising water; the brown; the blue . . . the blue wavy words. Quiet stay.

Suzanne came in and peeled the towel from Maya's eyes.

"Back in my country we only take Ayurvedic medicines," Maya told Suzanne, calmly, keeping it simple. She saw that there was a way out for her, a way to take back the indiscreet revelations she had made earlier, to give a better image back to the old lady who had brought forth her memories. Yes, she would give her something that would suit her idea of countries and cultures that had things easy with regard to health and healing.

"We have herbs to heal all things. When someone is sick, they are told to eat certain combinations of vegetables. All the vegetables have medicinal properties."

Suzanne, her eyes closed, inhaled deeply beside her. The strength of her exhalation brought a slow, warm touch of air that fluttered about Maya's face.

Suzanne's eyes shone with gratitude. "So lucky," she said.

Sleeping Alone

I want you to know that the first time I did anything, I told myself that I was simply playing. The way a magician might fade and find a coin out of habit, just to return to something familiar. I wanted them all, including Tusker, to suffer some easily remedied discomfort. Long hours before I recommended the turmeric and milk. They must have called their doctors, applied useless lotions squeezed out of tubes. I liked picturing all of it. I wallowed in how it all felt to me, that silent, lonely, despicable act perpetrated against people who called themselves my friends in that way Americans have of swilling sacred concepts in their mouths like they mean no more than mouthwash.

But I knew I was lying to myself: running away had not fixed me.

Still, I wish the boy hadn't come. I want to believe that if he hadn't been there, things would be different. I would have contented myself with small interruptions to the ordinary days of my new life among new and dispensable people in this haven of my own creation. What his particular disorder was I could not tell, only that his tongue thickened his words and that his hands felt swollen like some improbable bloom swaying on a thorny stem. It was at the Rachel Carson conference and I was just a last-minute add-on to *manage the small children*, the smallest accompanied by parents, though really they just should have had the good sense to leave them home. Every now and again one of them would walk over to me so I could pin paper cutouts of fruit and vegetables onto two maps to indicate origin: one for America and one for the world. America, of course, took up as much space on her map as did the entire world that included America on its. He slipped off his mother's lap, this boy, Adrian, his name tag declared, and came to me, his pudgy face too young for a six-year-old boy. I had knelt down to take his poorly colored paper fruit, a single orange—the colors racing off in jagged smears outside, way outside, the lines—when he did it. He dropped his paper and he put his palms over my face; his fingers spread apart, slowly, and the tips of his fingernails grazed my eyelashes, so I shut my eyes. He examined my face from my hairline to my chin, but not like a lover would, with just the fingers; Adrian used his entire hand. It made me quiet inside, as though I was in a deep meditation, revealed yet safe so long as his hands stayed on my skin.

"Brown . . . ," he said, with great effort, and the word was round and deep and loved in his mouth.

He waited for me to open my eyes, and perhaps because he saw some tenderness in my expression, he pointed at the world map and asked in that same labored manner, "Where do you grow?" The quietness turned rotten like dead bodies in bad movies because I lied. I could tell he knew I was lying; there was resistance in that pointing palm when I took it in mine and redirected it to the red-, white-, and blue-edged map.

I couldn't forget him, you see, which is how I knew that I had failed. I had not escaped; I had simply taken my habits with me. He had seen beneath the façade and that place was dangerous for me. I longed for it, for that sight, but on my own terms. Not by surprise, not like this, not complicated by innocence.

Today, having woken up the fifth morning in a row with the

sensation of two young palms upon my face, sometimes caressing me, sometimes suffocating me, I know it. I am no longer safe and it is time to leave.

You won't understand; you who are not me. I came alone to this country and finished growing up instantly; family is what family does, and there are enough aunts and uncles among the shoals of immigrants and refugees lumped under a single misnomer, Indian, Arab, Latino, you choose, to make one feel not merely at home but positively stifled by kin. I had done what I had to do, never mind that I stumbled upon it accidentally, or that They frightened me just as much as I, or an imaginary version of me, frightened other people. There was enough anger in me to help me overcome any aversions I may have had. There always is. You don't know the uncommon hatreds I carry behind my acquiescences. I am the slim, slivered bone that buries itself in an unreachable part of your throat, just when you thought the chowder tasted good. Yes, there *is* a price for demanding a pound of my flesh, cut close to the heart, to flavor your palate.

I stop at the Dunkin' Donuts for blueberry muffins and an American coffee. I ask for cream. I pay with my new Mastercard. Price of cream in my Dunkin' Donuts coffee? Bloating. Price of pork? Diarrhea. Feeling of bliss doing either? Priceless.

My companions in this town say I'm a closet Muslim. I was a Muslim in my past life, or will be in my next. I'm okay with that. I pass. I tell them I have recently started reading the Qur'an and reciting Arabic words aloud off the internet. And, I belly dance. *So well, with almost natural talent*, my teacher intones religiously, waiting for me to protest, which I, equally religiously, do.

I ask her to put my muffins in a box.

"We don't do boxes for six. We used to," she adds, helpfully, "a long time ago. Way back when I started here, we did them. About six years ago."

"I wasn't here six years ago," I say, and look into the distance, which isn't far because the post office is right across the street and it's a big one. Why do small American towns have such imposing official edifices? My *Thank God* hangs in the air.

"What?"

We lock eyes. "I wasn't here six years ago, so I wouldn't know." She looks carefully at my face. Does she wish I hadn't come, wouldn't stay, cluttering up her landscape, reminding her of other places and cultures she will never understand? Perhaps she wonders if I learned my English at the Let's Talk Language School on Main Street.

I drive off with what I consider to be verve, but the verve is hampered somewhat by the narrow curb-edged space between the Dunkin' Donuts and Main Street. From stocking books at Index on Seventh Avenue to . . . well, life in a Main-Street-having kind of town. In central Maine.

I'd been doing well: somewhere to sleep each night, beautiful hair, almost-American teeth, people who went with me to take in whatever came free or almost in the city, a job among books. My problems arose from what I loved best: kites. A vice so innocent and childlike, and so divergent to the harm I began to do to bring each one of them home. Premeditated, carefully executed acts that I became used to, after a while; the way what I did tapped into the existential crises that bubbled and froze and fell apart in shards inside my own body, slashing my character, making my insides cry. I had grown cruel living as I did, unseen and unknown. Not in the way people see and know you among the trees and houses planted in the country of your birth. Then again, this particular nation is particularly blind. It became not so bad after all, taking orders from people I would never meet, carrying them out without qualms.

But when he walked into the bookstore, I had seen a way out. In retrospect, maybe that was unfair: to ask a man to be an escape route from things he could not know, even if he had been named Tusker after some East African beer produced at a brewery his father had visited in Kenya a long time ago. A side run while on safari.

—

I'm at Marty's. This unabashed salvage store is what has, for the last two years, made life on Livacoc Avenue, Turlow, bearable, especially now that they have consolidated all three salvage stores into one gigantic diorama of bargains. I come here for designer clothes and snappy jewelry scooped off the shelves of some sad bankrupt store, or rescued from the rising flood waters of bayou towns. I can't help but linger in less innocuous aisles, among poisons and toxins, mostly to remember, sometimes to imagine what I can inflict.

The doors haven't opened yet. I park and have breakfast. A still blue day. It had been on a day like this that I had decided to buy the three gallons of generic cleaning solvent with its quantity of n-hexane. I had come here with the intention of buying mini paper umbrellas for the mixed drinks at our pool party, but I'd made an additional purchase. Mostly because Tusker had said: "Sameera, do you want to plan my annual pool party? You can do whatever you like. It can be a Moroccan thing. Or, like . . . what was that place you told me about once? Sheikh something or the other?"

"Sharm el-Sheikh. You should be able to say it by now, given how many international peace conferences have been held there."

"Of course, the City of Peace."

"You want me to re-create Sharm el-Sheikh in your backyard?"

"Oh, even you could never do that, honey! I just mean, you know, get a theme or something going with that in mind."

A theme, he had said. A theme! Out of a city that had been captured and recaptured and passed between nations like a precious gem and whose people had spent decades in the not-so-distant past living not in their Sharm el-Sheikh but in someone else's Mifratz Shlomo.

So I had nodded and, as I stood there, watching him, my eyes calm, my mouth relaxed, the lush brilliance of fiery coral reefs came up inside me, higher and higher, from the dark of the Red Sea. And, along with the memory, and counter to its upward movement, I had felt my feet beginning to slide into sin. The same sensation I'd had when I dove as a child in those waters, seeing my way along the nearly vertical cliff that dropped 2,500 feet down to the ocean floor.

A theme party around a pool in a backyard in central Maine, eh? I gave them a party so exquisite that months later they could not disentangle their enjoyment from a pain they could never associate with me. Salads with avocados and olive oil and onions and chick-peas, a cold beet and fennel soup, lamb kebabs slathered in goat curd and sumac made at home from hard dried fruits bought by the ounce online, almond bracelets, and, just to make them squirm, mihallabiya with extra rosewater. I watched them gag and reach for more almond cookies. *Ooh, try dipping the cookies in the pudding!* they exclaimed to one another. *Do people eat it that way in your country, Sameera?*

"It's a sweet after all. We can't be oppressed by our desserts, can we? There's no proper way. Sweet things can be eaten any way you like." And it put them at ease, that way I have of not-answering, not-judging. They laughed and felt understood.

And that meal, those drinks, all prettied up for them, the alcoholic ones as well as those I'd created, the fruit lassis and raspberry mint coolers, delighted them, made them want to leap in and out of the pool where the solvent lurked, disguised by water made blue by the tiles.

It was, I suppose, too bad that the spouses, students, and other invited guests with whom I had no specific bone suffered too, but I liked seeing that red irritation spread across their white skins like blood. Tusker fired the gardener and had to bring in some expert pool person to rebalance the pool. That's what he said.

"We need to get this pool rebalanced, Sameera, and I don't want you stepping in there until that's done."

"I won't. Is the rash any better?"

"Yes, it is. Thanks for that tip about the turmeric and whole milk in the bath. I told the others too. They were so grateful." He hugged me.

Tusker likes to talk to me as if I'm some unwanted girl he has rescued from a patriarchal society. He's actually forgotten the semi-truthful orphan story I fed him over our first mai tai at some fancy place he took me to. He's turned me vanilla. We used to do it in public places—that's my thing. All over New York City, where else? But since we moved, it's strictly in the bedroom and most frequently in the missionary position. I think Tusker would prefer it if I toned down the low-rise jeans and plunging necklines. I think he would like me to be brilliant yet unheard, quietly gracious, an Asset rather than a Force. So I say, "I bought a vibrator from Stacey at dance class."

"You . . . you . . . used?" he corrects himself, pulling away and watching me watching him.

"No, not used, factory sealed. I bought it at her pleasure party."

"Pleasure party?" He gives me one of those hmm-nods, the lips turned down, the brow slightly creased, a that's-different-I'm-a-liberal nod.

"It's a party where all the girls gather and pleasure each other . . ." I wait. He's still listening, believing, one palm on the counter, his weight on that side like he's holding off on a stroke until I'm finished. That, or keeping it from landing across my face. "It's just a party," I say, giving up. "Just a party where we can buy stuff like lingerie and massage oils and vibrators."

"Oh."

And that was all.

So, after the feel-good wore off, watching their skin pique and color uniformly, their confused eyes brushing repeatedly over my legs and belly and arms, my body all dressed for swimming in an orange polka-dot bikini and not a drop of water on it, all of them try-ing not to scratch and still, even at this point, unable to keep their hands off my food, my drink, I tried to occupy myself a little differ-ently, to let things be, to say this place is safe. Boring, yes, but safe.

But then I met that boy. He didn't know how I existed, poised between two types of dark: the benign and the malignant. And how once I'd known and fled the latter, I was a contaminant that could never really be comfortable with the former, just letting it be, considering it a reasonable price to pay for safety. I had tried to make it work, this time with Tusker and all that he could not give me. I had tried to hide my head, if not like an ostrich in the sand, then at least like a Canada goose in the blueberry patches. But it was useless. The boy couldn't see the whole of it, but he knew I was lying and that was going to trip me up sooner rather than later.

Leaving means destruction. Except, this once, I will be in charge.

———

You want to know who he is, this Tusker? Tusker Harris. Recently divorced professor of Middle Eastern studies, aged fifty-one. He walked into Index, and because he didn't say Tusker Harris, because he said Mr. T. Harris when he introduced himself to me, and be-cause that made him sound like a rap star (had I not been quite so desperate, I would have noticed that he wasn't young enough or cool enough and had too much hair on his head to be one), I picked him. I stood up on a stepladder in plain sight of where he was and reached for air just so I could present my best feature to him at eye level. At the counter, I murmured my thanks in Arabic, one of many languages in which I was fluent, because I could tell that a man holding a book that size about Islam would be a sucker for it. He drove the economy-sized U-Haul all the way to central Maine.

Well, okay, not that fast. First I had to repay O for all the advances he had given me for my kites. I'm not talking ordinary by-the-dozen-from-Oriental-Trading-Company kites, you understand. These were works of art that their makers did not want to part with and had to be pried loose from their souls and carried away with reverence, slowly, slowly, and backward, like drawing blood from a thin vein. I know about that, too, veins, specifically other peoples' veins, veins of left relatives in nursing homes, for instance, people whose deaths could be grouped together the same way the newsmen group the dead from other countries: Deacon Jones, New York City firefighter turned lieutenant killed in fighting in Basra, for instance, and, somewhere else, in a single line, this, for the rest of us: twenty-nine Iraqis were killed in the fighting. Yes, I knew about veins and not what I withdrew but what I put in them; in my other life when I was paid to wear a uniform and end lives, not save them.

My first real kite had been a gift from a "cousin" visiting from Tacoma Park, Maryland, which he called "hobo universe," a reference I found to be somewhat ironic considering that it cost a pretty packet to live there and acquire the American affectation of a hobo complete with Persian rugs on the wall and exotic creepers falling over wrought iron railings, while one stayed clean with French milled soaps, was into aromatherapy, and ate organic asparagus at $6.99 a pop. Shaul took me with him to buy the supplies from Chinatown, where he got genuine Mozi- and Lu Ban–worthy smiles from the proprietor when he asked for bamboo and tissue paper. I saw Shaul bring the kite to life, and that seduced me. The materials, the arch of his back bent over the work. I was fifteen and I fell in love.

There was nothing I wouldn't do to find the money I needed to buy kites like that from people whose distinctive touch and art

I learned to see in the snap and twist of their kites. At first I took loans. But I was only buying time. Somewhere down the line, actual money needed to enter the picture. Shaul found the work; well, let's say he trained me by outsourcing his assignments until I was good enough for my own. I never met my fixers; Shaul was the go-between. Maybe he was caught and kept just like I was. I didn't care for their causes, but I had stored up just enough resentment to ripen my innards for what I had to do. Just enough of it to comply, but not so much as to make me reckless. My need was simple: an untraceable side hustle. Bathed in the innocence of my addictions—and who can say if my addiction was just another lie I used to absolve myself—I was perfect. Until I wasn't.

I came to work that day tired of it all: my perpetual state of alertness; the endless searching of faces, places, street corners; the inability to trust anybody at all, not even the ticket machines at Penn Station. Sick of small acts of sabotage conducted usually in the broad light of day, in high-vis vests, the very fact of which was our best defense. It had seemed grand, briefly, when Shaul first recruited me, but after a while it was just another errand. Nothing changed: no headlines about food poisoning, about arterial blockages in the labyrinthine transportation systems in and out of NYC, sudden deaths of middling people, not even the mass deaths in nursing homes. Americans are too good at self-delusion and for calling reality fantasy and vice versa. There was no kick, eventually, for peons like me. Unless we were planning to disappear more people than we cared to, we were not going to be the small leaks that brought down the big ship. We were merely scratching at a steel hub, small fish beating our fins against an aircraft carrier. A depressing thought.

Tusker walked in.

People like me don't need preambles. We turn our feet where

they need to go, leaving behind or taking in, it's all the same to us. It is how we survive.

Tusker likes the color of my not-tanned-but-real-brown skin, my black hair, my preference for nose rings and waist chains and anklets that make follow-me noise. They make me exotic, I make him interesting. Who can blame him for wanting that? A quarter century in academe could do that to a person, make him want to possess something real from Over There, that region he visits and visits and even calls home by accident but that never celebrates his attention the way he thinks it should. The Middle East. Only Americans could conceive of teaching classes about the Middle East, as though it were some kind of days-of-yore folk tale from the past, a sort of Hollywood version of a Tolkien fantasy, only in mumbo-jumbo lingo that sounds like it means something. As if men on camels, AK-47s, and oil wells are the whole story. As if henna and zills are irrelevant.

You have to give me this: I tried to make Tusker see what he had in his home, to whom he had given refuge, could even keep.

"Don't you want to know how I afforded those kites?" I asked him. We were sitting at opposite ends of the living room couch, his feet on my lap, mine propped up on the coffee table, my toes warm from the fire, my palms around a cup of tea, two sugar cubes on a saucer on the armrest to my right.

"Hmm?" he said, his eyes lifting toward me, his fingers curling over his kept page.

I read the spine, vertically: *The Arab Mind*. Raphael Patai. I should have given up right then, but I pressed on: "My kites. Do you want to know how I got them?"

"I thought you said you bought them."

"I did. How else would anybody get kites like mine?"

"You borrowed money. I know, I helped you pay it back." I stayed silent a long time, which must have told him something even if it was the wrong thing because this is what he said: "You don't owe me anything, honey. You shouldn't feel bad about it. That's over. Done with. I wanted to give you the money. I wanted you to come with me as soon as possible, remember?" He wiggled his toes against my breasts.

He failed. I had too. He had been a wrong choice. I turned to him and smiled. I took one palm off my cup, pressed his feet, as if in fondness, and moved them away from my chest, my heart. He went back to his book after resettling his shoulders, nestling deeper into the already deep cushions. I put a cube of sugar in my mouth and held it between my teeth, let the tea pour through, sweetening itself, dissolving the sweetness, everything together and apart.

⁓

Today, a single morning after, I have a new plan for the Department of Middle Eastern Studies, with its faculty of four and one administrative assistant. That would be me, the assistant. Tusker finagled that. Thanks to him I have had the great joy of listening to Jess Boulus blather on about the impact of migrant labor on the domestic culture of Saudi Arabia, Pat Mather talk about Arab-Americans in the metropolitan cities of North America, Sylvain Q. Roberts (one is never allowed to forget that *Q*), teach archaeology and rudimentary Arabic, and Tusker, oh he of little faith, expound about Islam, all of whom have learned everything they know from books and from their five-star hotel visits overseas, all of whom fawn over me. Four white men holding down the rag that is called Middle Eastern Studies.

The Middle East, for those of you who might care to know, consists of parts of northern Africa, southwestern Asia, and southwestern Europe. It contains Bahrain, Cyprus, Egypt, Iraq, Iran, Jordan,

Kuwait, Lebanon, Oman, Qatar, Sudan, Saudi Arabia, Syria, Turkey, the United Arab Emirates, and Yemen. And we are not a unified bloc. Most of all, it contains Palestine, which means it contains Israel, which is carved from the insides of living bones.

Because none of them ever acknowledge the magnitude of all of that, I pick them for my send-off. In one week the new building opens. There's a dedication, a reception to follow. That is when I will do it, at the reception, but how?

Inside Marty's there's the usual arrangement: middle-aged women crowding the clothing aisles, middle-aged men in furniture trying out sectionals and avoiding the mirrors, old women stocking up on food, old men fingering batteries and hiking boots. At all times there are at least a dozen people looking up, scanning the store for their partners, some bargain in their hand that they wish to show off. At all times there are at least as many replacing the item and shuffling on down the rows of stuff, hoping perhaps to be closer to their other half the next time around; it was a bargain, but not worth lugging. I am always alone. Tusker has never been to Marty's.

I am drifting casually toward the household-goods section, open to being stopped by any possibility, when I come across the bin of real kites. There is nobody near it. It's only April; in Maine people are practical.

I think about the kites I have used to decorate the unfinished attic in Tusker's house. It was the first time I was able to have them all visible in a single space. I was fleetingly grateful to him for that. I am again. I like the way they hang up there, colorful aliens in an alien tomb, only moving when I open the trapdoor and climb in to sit with them for a while, tea in my hands, sugar clenched between my teeth, bundled up against the cold in the one-piece bunny pajamas Tusker got me. I like their menacing presence. All that unmoving color suspended in the darkness. I own twenty-nine of them, most of them purchased in the three years before I met

Tusker. Yes, he gave me money, Tusker did. I only had to ask once. He thought I was repaying student loans. I wasn't. I was making them, buying time. The trick was skipping town without my fix-ers finding out where I had gone; Tusker mistook my speed for ro-mance. The kites were a sideshow to him. He let me pack them into the back of that U-Haul, commenting on the care I took, indulging me and them as if I were a hippie and they were hippie art, represen-tative of an era but in poor taste.

But here I stand now in Marty's, kite upon kite tossed together as deliciously, as irreverently as a spiky tropical fruit salad! They are made in South Africa, priced at $5.99 apiece. I paid more than $600 for every single one of my kites, all but that first one Shaul gave me for free. For free except for the work I did for his friends in the city who didn't know what *eclectic* and *organic* meant but simply embodied both ideas as they went about their business, serving hot dogs, couriering letters, hauling heavy packages deliv-ered at work sites; in short, building America brick by conversa-tion by ketchup- or mustard-covered bun. Breaking it down, too, if forced, which is where I had come in, poised between two types of fear: of staying, of leaving.

There are arch-top diamonds, and Indian fighter kites that fly so easily in medium winds. I pick one up to feel perfection in my hands: featherweight. The cross spar is made of split bamboo and balances with no effort at the tip of my middle finger on its cen-ter point. Its tassels drape gracefully from the sides. The diamonds have tails clearly made by a master crafter. One hundred fifty feet of string with each kite. Five dollars and ninety-nine cents?

The man who stops at the bin is tall, with a confident stare. Pale blue eyes, though, the untrustworthy, watery kind.

"You fly kites?" he asks, a pre-smile upward promise lingering along the corners of his mouth.

"No," I say, before I can stop myself. "I collect them."

"Collect them! What for?"

I think fast. "It's something to collect, right? People collect teddy bears. Teaspoons. I collect kites." Also books, I want to add. I do collect books, and dust along with the books. "You don't need as many to make the lot look good." I give him The Smile. His vanishes. He narrows his eyes. I'm intrigued.

"You must know kites well, then. You think this one will fly?" he asks, picking up a fighter, his neck bunching on one side as he tilts his head, mouth pursed. He reminds me of people in uniforms, their smug, lazy manner, obviously not charmed by me. I stay calm. What would a man in uniform want, or do, with the partner of a college professor in a college town?

"They'll all fly—it depends on whether you know how to fly them."

"A kite's a kite after all."

"Yes, but not all kites are meant to fly. These kites are, but some are meant for other things, like decorations, gifts." I think about those first Chinese kites measuring distance, the role they played in moving armies. "Even letters," I add.

"Letters?" The neck re-collects on the other side.

"You know, communication between people who are not allowed to talk to each other, for instance. You can send messages."

"In-ter-esting," he says, and he looks carefully at my face, like and unlike the boy who haunts me. That question again, the force of it: "Where are you from?"

I look at his well-used hands, the angle of his hat, the boots. I am tempted, but his shirt stops me. It is crisp, ironed and in a solid color. Men who are harmless don't wear solid-colored shirts. That was one of the rules I had learned back when I needed to know whom I could trust, whom I could use. "New York," I say, "but I live here now. My husband teaches at the college." I slide my left hand underneath the kite before I say that, anticipating the glance.

His eyebrows rise together. He nods. "Originally?"

"Yes, New York."

"What does he teach?"

"Religion," I say, smiling again. This time he smiles back.

I wonder what he imagines, probably something involving slides of stained-glass ceilings and cathedrals in Rome. Certainly not prayer mats or men wheeling in great rings, white robes ballooning around them. Like angels.

"Which one should I get?"

"Who will be flying it?"

"My son." He looks up at me. "He's five."

No five-year-old could fly these kites the way they are meant to be flown, but I can't tell him that. I can only select one no American boy born to a father like him would want to fly. I examine several and pick out a pink-and-green kite. More pink than green. I hand it to him.

"This one."

He takes it from me and turns it around from side to side, looking for a flaw, or perhaps a distinguishing mark that separates it from the rest.

"Are you sure?"

"Yes, like you said, I know kites. This is the best of them all."

He nods his thanks and moves away, leaving me to stare at the bin. I stare and stare until it comes to me: the plan. Oh, they would have been proud of me had they known. It isn't truly satisfying to perform these acts of suicide without anybody to witness them. It's like foreplay without the sex. My life is all foreplay these days, secret, tumultuous, desirous, and unfulfilled. But it could be worse. I could be dead or discovered. I'd prefer the former over the latter with all its American-style hysteria.

I pay in cash.

———

I wear red. Nobody suspects anybody in red of anything but shame-lessness. They are right on that count; I have no shame. My life with Tusker is all the proof they would need of that; if only they weren't blinded by his distinguished looks and his money and my exoti-cism and assumed allegiances. *Of course* She would be attracted to Him. *Of course* He would want to bring Her home. We are both, uniquely, trophies in this world, a winning combination of intellect and authenticity. The trouble with this equation being that we are taken for a Venn diagram whose circles intersect only in bed. But I know that Tusker shares my disdain for his nation of fools, that he loves my nation of fools more passionately sometimes than I do; our only difference being that his version draws the line at doing some-thing about his hates and his loves. Mine requires action for, with, against, about, you choose. My nation of fools despises inertia; his thrives on it. His prefers carpet-bombing. Mine prefers carpets. His rains fire from above. Mine lays traps underground. His struts on a stage with fanfare and the national anthem screamed, badly, always badly, into microphones. Mine moves behind wisps of cloth, whis-pers prayers deep into the heart of the earth. His unleashes torna-does that weathermen plot for months ahead and usually get wrong. Mine erupts in earthquakes that nobody sees coming. But we share our bed and our prejudices.

I wear red.

They all agreed to the idea of releasing the kites. Why? Because I told them it was *a custom*. The Department of Middle Eastern Studies believes those they consider to have cornered the market on authentic traditions just by virtue of a little melanin. Americans, above all, are afraid to offend in person, unlike us Others who vil-ify in person but welcome strangers with open arms.

"In many small villages in the Middle East, it is traditional to release kites into the air on a day of celebration," I said. Everybody agreed that this would be a splendid addition to the festivities. Nobody asked me the obvious: Which parts? Which villages? Why?

They only asked me if I could find out where to get kites, and should they call the local papers? Yes, of course, to both.

"Marty's has them. I can pick them up."

"Don't forget to submit the receipt," they said, which complicated it all a little because I had to return the kites I'd already bought to Marty's and then buy them again with the correct date imprinted on the receipt.

"Oh, I just wanted different colors," I said, when the customer service lady asked, thankful that she was used to that from me.

Everything looks perfect when I stop in at the Lakin-Alder-Setzer House, or LASH, as I prefer to call it, named for the people who gave all the money for the new digs for our department. The benefactors are the alumni-parents of two protégés belonging to Pat Mather and one rather soulful boy owned by Tusker. Pat, it is generally known, thinks that he has the real claim to fame in the department, particularly after those two decapitated towers sank to the ground like cakes with too much leavening. Oh, he had quite the run on NPR back then, quoted here, quoted there, misquoted elsewhere, called to testify about everything under the sun from one coast to the other, all because he knew about "Arabs" and their doings in American cities. He dropped out of favor, though, after they rounded up the sleeper cell upstate that one time. Even I felt sorry for him. He kept trying to insist that there were no sleeper cells outside the cities but nobody believed him. Only I did, though I couldn't say, because I know.

I know where the cells are.

I know what kind of person belongs to them.

I know that most of us have the same tired dreams on our quasi-American minds.

I know that sleep eludes the hired zealot.

I know we are not zealous about much else besides survival. Same as anyone else.

Downstairs in the foyer of the new building, there's staff from dining services milling about. That's inconvenient.

"Hello, Sameera!" That's Kerri, the head of the waitstaff. I like Kerri. She is not that much taller than I am, but she's round from neck to thigh. It is vital to have people like that sprinkled throughout the food service industry. Who wants to be served by thin people? Besides, she's Irish and crinkly around the eyes and she loves me. She always sends the servers my way at these functions, particularly the ones with crab cakes, and pours me my drinks without my having to ask her for them. Vodka with passion fruit and salt. Always.

"Hi, Kerri! Everything set for tonight?"

"Take a look dear, what do you think?"

I've already seen, but I look around anyway. "Beautiful, Kerri, just beautiful. You do such great work."

"You all ready with something gorgeous to wear tonight?"

I nod. She squeezes my upper arm and walks away, her head swiveling from left to right, taking things in, assessing, directing. I stand there to watch her disappear through the wide-open doors and down the steps to the truck parked outside. I imagine the boy walking out behind her. I want them to leave this place together, this sole woman for whom I have developed a fondness, and the boy with his knowing hands. I picture them safe. For a few moments I let myself go back in time: I am standing before two maps, I answer the boy truthfully, show him where I was born, and know that it is all right, that I will not harm anyone because I have the choice not to. For a few moments I am not complicit in the crimes of his country or mine, nobody owns me, I am free.

After a while, Kerri comes back.

"What are you still doing here, dear?"

"Oh, I've forgotten something," I say. "I'm hoping I'll remember if I stand here long enough."

"Want a little taste of this?" she asks, and lifts the silver cover on a platter. Inside are reddish-brown sweet-and-sour meatballs glistening in gravy. She skewers a meatball, then holds it up until I open my mouth. She uses the same toothpick to put one in hers. We stand there, our cheeks bulging, enjoying the particularly delicious taste of stolen food. She reaches over to wipe the corners of my mouth when I'm done.

"Good, wasn't it?" she asks.

I put my arms around her and hug myself to her.

"Oh, you are a sweetheart," she says, somewhere near the top of my head. I nod, squeeze her tighter one last time, then let her go. She chucks me under the chin, wipes her hands on her apron, fixes a few things on the table. I watch her walk out of the building once more.

I continue to stand, trying to let these two people, Kerri, the boy, their lives, invade my plan, but they remain just outside reach. I go to the van to unload the kites.

Urushiol oil. Who would guess? The common name for it, found on the labels tacked onto bottles of soothing creams, and on the lips of anxious mothers, sounds almost fairylike: poison ivy. Yes, harmless, mostly, like everything else in small doses. It's when things accumulate, reach a critical mass that life begins to break down. Then one needs just the proverbial straw. Or, in my case, a little something extra.

I wear one of my skin-protecting suits. It's a leftover from that previous life when self-protection was how we dismantled the lives of others. Sometimes it was mere stealth, the removal of a camera, the insider-on-our-side. Other assignments called for armor of one sort or another. This one is all black, sleek, easy to cover up with ordinary sweats and a long-sleeved shirt. I tuck my legs into gum boots that rise above my knees, slip on three pairs of those easy-breezy disposable gloves. Simple to find the dark, shiny patches of poison, simple to lay those strings down and stamp the strings into the leaves, a particularly furious grind for Tusker. For having been the one to effect my rescue yet not having had the intuition to understand me, to coax my confidences. What use is a secret if nobody knows you keep one?

Once I'd worked up a good sweat, I pick them up, tenderly, and arrange them, one on top of the other, their poisoned strings coiled around their respective bits of wood. I discard my gloves to put on a different, impermeable pair. I adjust my mask. I pick up the slim beaker of ricin. Afterward, I stack the kites inside the plastic bag I had made. Crouched inside the attic, I seal the edges with the flame of a candle, with my own beautiful kites looking on. It feels positively religious to me, this secret time. The way the colors dance in and out of the frames around my head and along the floor in the light of the single candle, the thin smoke from the singed plastic, the way it feels under my fingers, hot, then warm, then cold, almost instantly.

I leave them, still sealed, in full sight on the round linen-draped table set aside for the purpose. Then I go home to dress.

—

By afternoon, the weather is perfect: the occasional jet trail cross-stitching the lapis lazuli skies, a brisk gusty wind that can carry man-made flying things. The food is perfect: stuffed mushrooms, fancy crisped pita triangles with silky hummus, meats wrapped in prosciutto, delicate pastries, cheeses arranged in circles next to bowls of fresh olive tapenade and elegant crackers, bundles of luxuries tucked into grape leaves. Very good wine. I feel perfect; perfect, impenetrable, completely above suspicion. The silk gloves were a stroke of genius. Just in case.

I'm standing on the wraparound veranda of the building when I hear the voice at my elbow.

"Red suits you," it says. It's the man from Marty's, all cozy as if I myself had invited him to attend the celebration. "Newsman," he says, holding up a pen (and no paper that I can see), in explanation.

I nod, my eyebrows raised in a proper demonstration of admiration.

"It's a good day to be out of the office," I say, smiling that smile again, to better effect this time; it's probably my clothing, the high heels, perfume. Men, wherever you find them.

"Indeed," he says, looking out over the grass at the crowds on the lawn, then turning back to me, "and for kites."

"I don't think you're going to be allowed to fly any this evening." I touch him, flat palmed, fingers together on his upper arm, consoling, flirting. American men like that sort of intimacy from women they believe are too demure to touch strange men. They think it means we cannot, simply cannot, hold back our desire. I can sense I don't yet have him on my side, despite the pleasure on his face.

"No, but I'll be writing all about it tomorrow."

Tusker comes up. "Sameera, they're looking for the kites," he says, glancing at the man but not really interested in an introduction, which irks me, so I say, "This is . . . what's your name?"

Again, that smile. "Samuel Herbst. Sam," he says.

"Sam, this is Tusker Harris, my husband."

This time Tusker looks at me, confusion in his eyes. "Well . . ." He laughs here, nervous, condescending. "Not yet, but soon." He pats my hand. I am glad that he will fly at least one of those kites later this evening. Deeply glad.

Sam looks at me with that same tilt-headed glance he'd used to try to see through me at Marty's. I add the slow, knowing, up-down to his head that he does not actually articulate.

"Soon, yes," I say. I feel it beginning to uncoil inside my body, the thing that I knew would come, that I wanted: flight. I look back at Sam, regretfully, so he'll remember my regret, and address him, not Tusker: "On the table outside. The kites are there."

"Well, I guess it's time for the show," Sam says. He rubs his palms together.

"I guess so."

It is poetic justice that the wind kicks up with such sudden immediacy that the kites are lifted and carried away effortlessly; as though the heavenly sky wants to save them. I hope the wind is laughing at how hard they hold on against that divine effort, how much they want to prolong this authentic, ethnic moment, each inch of that string sloughing off poison as it moves through their acquisitive fists. I stand with my arm looped through Tusker's just to give the impression that I had been present in equal measure, lifting my face up in a fiasco of joyful participation so nobody would notice that I touched nothing.

Afterward, I see Kerri behind the serving dishes as I walk back inside. Her hands are covered up to her elbows in the transparent gloves of the waiting staff. This serendipity delights me. I smile and wink at her. She smiles back at me and turns to listen to some request. Mrs. Boulus is asking for more spinach-and-feta pastries.

"Kerri, these are amazing. I've had six already!" she says.

"Have more, Mrs. Boulus." Kerri slides three pastries onto a paper plate.

I want Mrs. Boulus to leave. Leave Kerri alone, but she does not. She reaches over to touch Kerri's face. "You've got a crumb on your cheek, Kerri. Naughty, naughty." Then, because now she has added the grease from her own crumb-covered fingers to that face, she keeps rubbing, trying to undo the first mistake.

I freeze, but there is nothing I can do. I turn away.

Long after the kites have disappeared over the far trees and farther over the low hills beyond, I monitor the effects from the window of my new office. All I see are hands: long-fingered hands, short stubby paws, gnarled ones, young, elastic versions, neither-here-nor-there varieties, all moving, touching, stroking one another's exposed skins, their own, the eyebrows, the upper arms, the smoothing-over-faces gestures, the fingers that touch and touch and touch everything—most significantly the food, the wine, the glasses, the plates. I stay away because I can no longer tell where they have spread the poison, or when it may reach me.

I hear the door behind me. The stillness tells me it is Sam, and that he is not a newspaper man. It tells me he has kept his distance, that I am vulnerable. Still, I do not flinch, because there is more that I can tell. It is in the air: this is a public place and as good as any to end this time, to give him something that will disturb his life and prevent his truths from surfacing. He is not a newspaper man, but he is a man. And I am a woman more skilled in these arts than any he could ever find in his universe of paper-bagged glossy magazines and underwear ads on TV. I carry my learning in the marrow of my bones, my practice in my mind; I come in layers like the sweets in my country of birth, the million threads in a single heavy carpet carried back as a souvenir for a preprogrammed love. So I do not move, I wait for him to draw nearer; I wait, motionless yet expectant, straight. I am unafraid. That is the first rule and the last.

Tonight, while this community begins to come apart, I will pray, aiming my body like an arrow toward the heart of God.

I will pray for that boy who had seen me as I had wished to be seen, who had placed me in the elsewhere in which I belonged.

After midnight, someone untouchable will come for me, because I have nobody else to tell. Someone will come for me, and I will go, back to that deeper darkness, taking my kites, my unharmed skin.

Retaining Walls

He wears a white shirt and wrinkle-free pants, usually khaki or some other color that reflects well on him. It's superstition, not good taste.

There is work during these summer months for Saul Morton, who, at thirty-nine years of age, and with a name like that, has disappointed his fair share of those women who approached him at a bar and pinned their hopes on a desk-job lover, never mind that he is married. Their expectations ruined in slow motion when he divulged the origin of his paychecks: contractor. He has long ceased blaming his parents, both educators. He has not, however, stopped wearing the crisp white shirts that his wife had once admired. A long time ago, when promise still hovered above them like a last summer sunrise and his occupation had seemed temporary.

People take him seriously when he appears in neatly pressed clothes, carrying his substantial portfolio. They feel he can liaise between them and the other men. The one who can bridge the morass of poor taste, bad calls, inferior workmanship, cheap materials, and just plain stupidity, and manage to present them with a house built to spec. Those that are truly wealthy don't care one way or another, really. They are free of the fetters of propriety, bank balances, and state-owned 529 plans. Tomorrow unfolds like today.

Their children go to college, their homes are never repossessed, they can and do terminate a contractor or even raze a house to the ground if they feel like it. He could appear in beach shorts for all they care. And yet, even to those meetings, he wears the white shirts, the wrinkle-free pants.

He wears them now as he stick-shifts his car down roads with a posted village speed limit of twenty-five miles an hour, preparing to meet the Stevensons.

"Er, this is a message for Mr. Saul Morton, the building contractor. This is Mr. Stevenson. We would like to set up a meeting for an assessment on our house. We're hoping to make some changes . . . what? . . . yes, additions . . . no, that's not now, we can talk about that later." The number, the name spelled out, twice.

The telephone conversation he had subsequently with Mr. Stevenson unfolded in the same way as his voice-mail message, with many interruptions and clarifications from Mrs. Stevenson. He had hung up saying that he looked forward to meeting them. He could picture them, long married, accustomed to the back-and-forth, to being corrected, to self-correcting in anticipation. It made him smile. He liked older couples. Liked the fact that they had lasted.

He chews on a splinter of wood as he drives the old red Ford pickup, spits the mouth mulch out of the window, and starts in on another piece before he reaches his destination. This habit maddens his wife. It must remind her of his livelihood, the simplicity of his background. He thinks about her each time he spits. Each time he resolves to stop. As usual, the implication of the resolution causes so much anxiety that he immediately reaches for another bit of wood. He rinses out his mouth with a swig of ginger ale from the fresh can in the drink holder and turns into the pretty suburban neighborhood.

Over twenty years at the same job in the same town he has

developed insights he keeps mostly to himself. Hope, he knows, is what keeps Home Depot in business: the hope of erasure, the anticipation of obliterating whatever dull taste has been acquired during hours more leaden than any that they had, himself included, ridiculed when they were sixteen-year-old potential sweethearts. Way back when they lay in each other's arms behind their high school bleachers, watching fireworks light up long-ago July skies, mirroring an imagined future. This shared delusion that the walls contain both blame and antidote is what prompts his clients to build.

If they are young, they will take a day trip to the faraway IKEA to help with the upgrade, a strenuous effort to strike the right note: toss out the old Billy, say hello to the Hemnes bookshelf; throw in the Strandmon wing chair and a Björksnäs nightstand and all of a sudden you got style. Their middle-class parents, only slightly above the children's price-range, updated kitchens with Akurum and Värde; the richer ones with Newfane Etagere display cases, Mission end tables, and couches custom made by the faraway-nearby Pompanoosuc Mills. An aspiration to being *more than* before, *more than* was expected of them, unifies the classes; rich or poor, they were mostly the same. Florence with art tours versus Caribbean cruises where bronze-level dancers with illusions of greatness taught the merengue, and people walked away thinking they had learned to dance. A cultivated preference for Stilton and *fromage bleu* versus Doritos in the weekly grocery cart. Different garnishes at Thanksgiving, but the same stuffed bird.

As far as he could tell, only older couples that remarry find lightness. The norm is always otherwise: for the glow of "home" to dim and sputter, to appear constrained at family gatherings. He knows this firsthand, has seen it in every house he has rebuilt. People lay the table for years for the children, never minding the kitsch. The kids enjoy it, they say, who cares what the neighbors think of the excessive yuletide spirit scattered around the lawn? But the children grow up, and then they find that what had been best for the children has become their style. The rich withstand it with a personal metamorphosis into a classier mode. Quick acquisitions that project a more contemporary image, herald a new stage. Remodeling that erases the past, but for carefully zoned arrangements of old photographs, preferably in black and white, where the extravagance of a purposeless $1,600 hallway bench turns a youngest into a social activist. A place where the visitors are comfortable but rarely stay. A construction of life that replaces the hearth with an Investment.

His own children will not visit either, of that he is sure, when they finally leave. It is the blight of those like him who start families at the age of twenty and raise children with aspirations greater than their parents could ever have. He has seen it happen in more than one house over the years. Too much remained the same. Those cheap-looking wind socks, the white plates with the blue maple-leaf patterns brushed along one side. Rooms that still seem to want to hold the ten-year-olds, not the lawyers, the publicists, the adult single people who come for the holidays because, they promise their significant others, it's just for a day, put up with it. The slanted corners irritate those children. Could happiness ever have been possible in these spaces? He has learned to read those unuttered judgments in the eyes of other people's children when he chances to meet them on-site. Their discomfort in their parents' comfortable houses: the way they shower only once during their stay, preferring not to engage with the rusty sliding doors in the bath; the way they bring most of their food with them in deli-packed disposable containers, the home cooking too provincial for their newly acquired tastes. He gazes at the American flag in front of the Stevensons' house, limp without its dance partner on that slow summer day, and pegs them as the burgeoning average.

The Stevenson home is an in-between. The kind he loves best. A small addition at the back, the owners flirting with retirement, building something they'd always hoped to have and now would perhaps enjoy for a year before selling the house, afraid of spoiling it with overuse. He can see the coming battles. The furrowed brows and the admonishments to grandchildren. Don't go there. Don't touch that. Don't. He notes the lines as he sits for a few minutes in the freshly sealed driveway. A haphazard sprawl of mismatched add-ons. He visualizes the succeeding waves of ownership, the house already almost a century old.

The couple come to the door, first Jack, then Ellen. They serve him tea and small jam tarts, one of her best recipes, he is told. He succumbs to the tour of the entire house. He listens to the stories that are contained around each corner: the one about the time Noah chipped the wood paneling when, at the age of twelve, he flung a rolling pin at it in exasperation with his first piecrust; the story of Leah, who streaked the tub a lemony green when she experimented with a homemade hair color; the place where Mary had etched all their names into the kitchen door frame.

"That was when Jack was laid off and we were on the brink of selling our home and moving to his mother's place the next town over," Ellen says.

They are the usual tales, but, as always, he responds to them as if he has never known such children before. His mind fills in the sensations, the colors and textures of their small history. There are no stories about the fourth child, Luke, though his name is written in calligraphy, along with those of his siblings, in the frame around the large family photo centered on the mantel. The omission is tangible. Saul observes the way the ethereal domesticity of Ellen's hands soothe her surroundings, caressing walls, bookcases, the banister, a child-made vase here, the silver-plated jug there on the sideboard. Ceaseless, insatiable—never arriving at the object of desire, the one touch that can make all the others unnecessary. Saul looks at Ellen, allows his eyes to reflect the sympathy he feels, invites her confidence. It's a gift he has, the way he can transform himself into an intimate, no matter the exchange of signed papers and checks, but he uses it sparingly.

"My other son is Luke. He left us," Ellen says finally.

Jack bows his head, and Saul can tell in the grip of his hand on the banister that there is more to the story than that.

When they show him the pull-down ladder that leads into the attic, Saul says, "I don't need to see it," but they insist. He follows Jack up the open rungs and is unsurprised at the sound of her step behind him. He wonders if he should turn around and help her but realizes there is no need. Ellen's strength and agility rival his. Her gait, careless and light, mocks his cautious elbow when she reaches the top. He looks at her and sees her smiling as she pushes hair out of her eyes. He is relieved, marveling at the change that has taken place between the stairwell and the attic. She has a delicate face, the sweetness of nursery rhyme mothers, only grayer. She must be sixty, he thinks, a full two decades older than he is. He's probably not much older than the son who has gone away.

The attic is, like their stories, cluttered with the ordinary small-town business of making a life. Remnants of woodworking projects, trunks and plastic bins full of the output of four children ascending through grade school. Old clothes gathered for the ever-possible yard sale. Items removed from their packaging, and in some cases from their motherboards, languish in disuse, their original intent forever a mystery. In a few neat corners, gift wrap, Christmas decorations, leftover wallpaper, and warehouse sale-priced rolls of toilet tissue and paper towels await their pedestrian demise.

Saul examines the beams, the insulation. He assesses potential. He sees the room collapse and reopen to light, glass-filtered sun flooding its length.

"Ma?" The voice is faint by the time it reaches them. Jack leans against the frame, his fingers fiddling endlessly with the change in his pocket, a sound Saul knows that Ellen no longer hears. He closes his eyes, suppressing the need to still those hands.

"I thought you said they would not be back till supper," Jack says weakly, as though he's struggling for air.

Saul offers his hand but Jack waves him off and begins the descent toward the voices on the landing beneath. He seems so much older than Ellen, who follows with the same brisk energy with which she had ascended earlier.

"What's going on, Ma? I thought you were going over to the Nawfels. We came back to clean up a little. Maybe let the kids take a swim and then close up the pool for you. It's getting chilly, Ma, don't you think? Time to close it down. Maybe we should have a last barbeque tonight? Noah got some corn on the way down. We didn't want to do all that driving back to Boston. Thought it would be a nice surprise. What do you say?"

The voice goes on in its singsong. She's a dark-haired, smiling woman, startlingly feminine in a gauzy orange dress and heels, out of place in that aging house. She reminds Saul of his own wife, that same determination to be youthful in her beauty. He thinks of how other men seem to envy him when they see him with her still, the same way other women are drawn to him. Why, then, do they no longer turn to each other with the same alertness? His fingers find a stray chip in his pocket and he caresses it, his fingers soft against the brittle wood.

She stands with her arm around Ellen. "Saul?" Ellen says. "This is my son Noah and my daughter-in-law Vivy. Vivy, Saul Morton. He's going to be working on the house. The addition, you know, I told you about it. Over by the dining room? We've always wanted a screened porch there and a deck out back. Never got around to it. Seems like it might be time now. Who knows, someone might want to move back home, right, Noah?"

Saul extends his hand, takes Vivy's. It is warm and generously affectionate, the way much-loved people extend themselves. Noah smiles and nods, but his arms are filled with a wriggling child.

Ellen points to the child, who seems almost too big for carrying. "That's Samuel, and the other two are Joshua and Anthony. My triplet grandchildren," she says.

They are identical and there is nothing of Noah in them. Saul can see the color rise in Ellen's face as she notices his gaze shift to the mantel and back. Luke's blond hair falls over their faces with the same beachy waves; Luke's blue eyes meet his, solemn and already troubled.

"You have beautiful sons," Saul says to Noah, and then he turns to Vivy, including her. "I better keep my daughters away from them." He relaxes into their laughter, listening hardest for Ellen's, which is infused with gratitude.

Jack goes over to the fridge and busies himself with a glass of milk.

"Grampy, can I have some?" Anthony ducks himself between his grandfather and the open refrigerator. Jack gets a glass, pours the boy some milk, and puts it on the counter. Anthony thanks the old man, smiles at him. Joshua stands next to his mother saying nothing, motionless, almost absent. Ellen watches him, her face loving, unearthly.

—

Ellen doesn't need convincing. Whatever Saul proposes, she approves. He begins with the attic. A smaller storage area at one end to contain shrinking accumulations as each daughter gathers what she wants to save for her own children, and the daughters-in-law—he allows the plural—will salvage what they can for theirs. He envisions a new space in the far alcove for Ellen, who has not asked for it.

"But is it necessary?" Jack asks. "There's other spaces that Ellen uses; we don't need an additional room here." His plaid flannel has begun to hang on him after a long flu. Ellen appears to have grown more robust by comparison.

"The boys might like to have a place to themselves one day, when they're teenagers," she says. "If we are able to manage it during this renovation, it'll already be there when they get to that age."

"In another seven years we'll have sold up and moved to the Keys," Jack murmurs, his weight on his arm, looking at the plans on the table.

"Perhaps," Ellen says, but when Jack is out of earshot, she speaks differently. "We will never sell. This is the home where all my children were born, the place Luke knew—" She leaves the thought dangling. Saul folds up the papers and turns the conversation over to considerations of light and colors and she comes along with him into that safe territory.

He opens up the interior; there are no more dead ends or useless corridors. The house turns interesting, its corners inviting. A family of six could gather easily when they want to, but find serenity in solitude if they prefer. From the living room window you can take in the neat front lawn, its cherry trees, the early spring whites of bloodroot and foamflowers, and the profusion of yellows among the marsh marigold, silverweed, and bluebead lilies to come later. In the back, a screened-in spare porch beyond the kitchen looks out at the trim beds of blue flag and harebell, their blue variations offset by Ellen's favorite, the obedient plant, aptly named, dark green leaved and flowering pink. He widens the windows on the front-facing rooms but adds landscaping that affords them privacy. They can sit there and regard the neighborhood.

"If only we had lived in this house that you are making, not the other one," Ellen says one day, joining Saul as he rests on one of the wooden benches that matches the precise shade of timber of the deck.

"Your old house had its own strengths," Saul says.

"We changed nothing about it. We hung our lives on existing bones. We painted the walls, we got new towels, that's all."

Saul shrugs. "That's all most folk manage. It's hard to do too much while raising kids, and you had four of them then."

"I have four," she says, and sips her coffee. A chorus of birds seems to chime in on the assertion. The rising note and the sharp chip at the end of a northern parula's song; further afield, the blurring drum of a hairy woodpecker.

Saul listens to the birds, and to the slight tap of Ellen's fingernails on her cup.

"Sometimes I wonder whether it was us who remained children, the two of us, Jack and I. Even the paint, that was the boys' doing. They moved forward. Noah wanted blue in his room. But Luke could never decide. White, yellow, even red. Whatever suited his mood. Sometimes in a single year. And the girls changed our place settings. Without them, we'd still be using the same dishes we bought at a flea market when we got married, and the same linens my parents gave us."

Saul nods. "My home is no different. For all the building I do for other families, my own house is unchanged."

There's a motion beyond a low hedge of lupines and both of them watch Jack as he tends to weeds. "Maybe it was I who never changed. Jack always had the garden. It was just grass when we bought the house. And now look at it. Every shrub and flower, every tree was planted by Jack. Except the weeping cherry. Luke planted that for me one year for Mother's Day."

"It looks well, given that it isn't suited for our zone."

"He was so optimistic. When he wasn't sad, that is. Always one or the other. He could have just as easily cut down that tree if someone else had planted it as plant it himself. People said he was angry all the time. But it wasn't anger, you know. He was just sad. I could never figure out what made him happy."

"Saul!" Jack calls out from around the house, and Saul hesitates, but Ellen gives him permission to leave with a movement of her head.

"He probably needs help with some root or a ladder or something. You carry on, Saul." She rests her palm on his shoulder briefly and goes indoors.

Sometimes as he works, Vivy and Noah visit. They are a partnership. They work together like trained athletes passing a baton, never dropping it, never looking at each other, simply running, keeping the white stick that brings them together airborne. There is a distance between them that Saul cannot ignore. The children flow seamlessly back and forth. Saul recognizes this dance. It is also his own. He thinks about his children—Emily, Andrew, Lilly, thirteen, eleven, nine. Their mother, his wife, their life that is as devoid of friendship, as perfectly orchestrated to create the illusion of solidity. For the children. Everything that is best for the children.

Mary visits one day in the summer and Saul is struck by the similarity when Ellen brings her over to introduce them. "The apple and the tree," he says when he shakes her hand, and they both laugh.

"Only in looks," Mary says. "I am never going to settle down like she did, do all this homemaking stuff." But she holds her mother close to her body with genuine warmth when she speaks.

"You will one day, when the right person comes along."

Mary rolls her eyes, inviting Saul to side with her. "There are no right and wrong people, are there, Saul? There is only chance and choice."

"Oh, I wouldn't say that. Some people are better than others for us. Look at your parents."

"One time in a million. I don't know any couples like them. I'd rather not play the lottery on the rest of my life. Besides, I've got hundreds of children."

"She's a teacher," Ellen says.

"Professor. I'm a professor."

Saul listens to the two women talk as they walk around the premises, and he can't help but wonder what Mary's sister is like, what Luke might have been like. He wonders if he will ever meet Leah, ever know what happened to Luke.

He stays for an early supper that day. It's a formal dinner in honor of Mary's visit, with Noah and Vivy and the children too. Saul feels an odd sense of belonging when he is seated next to Ellen at one end of the table, with Mary to his right. She is easy to talk to, an easy presence, blessed by the devotion of both parents. Unlike Noah, who has slipped away from them by his marriage to Vivy.

"They aren't married," Mary says to him as they put away the dishes. "That's why my father doesn't like her." And then, seeing the question in his eyes: "The kids aren't Noah's."

Saul nods. "I know. They're Luke's."

"Did my mother tell you that?" Mary says.

"No, they did. Their faces."

It is her turn to nod. "Yes. Nobody could hide Luke. Not then. Not now. His whole self. His tempers, but also his beauty. My brother was ethereal. Unlike the rest of us. He stood out. He did not look like any of us, or either of our parents. There were times I wondered where he came from. We would tease him, in that way siblings do when they are jealous. We would say that he was adopted, imply that he did not belong. There was a way Mama loved him especially hard, if that is possible for a mother like her, so devoted to the job of mothering. We were never excluded from her embrace, but he was more steady within it. We tried to escape it, but he stood still, as though it was his only refuge. Maybe it was."

Ellen comes in with a few stray plates that the children had left around the house. "I can finish up here, Saul. I'm sure you need to get home."

Saul looks past her at Mary, overcome with the urge to stay right there, in the presence of the assured and gracious woman who talks to him like she sees the man beneath the work that he does.

"I'll walk him out, Mama," Mary says, and continues talking about Luke as though they had not been interrupted. "It was hardest on her, the moods that fell on him like drapes, thick, impenetrable to us all. Even to her, except sometimes, and then, when she managed to break through, he was so grateful. It was no wonder she kept trying through all the worst times."

Before he leaves, she moves with ease into his embrace and stays there a long time. Still within his hold, she looks up and puts her palms on his face. "Luke killed himself. Please don't ever let my mother say those words to you."

In the darkness of his own house, Saul checks on his children. He touches the heads of each of his girls but does not linger. He kneels instead by his son's bed and watches him sleep. He considers sleeping on the floor beside him, but does not; it would reveal all the things that children pretend they do not know. He gets up and goes to his own bed, where his wife has fallen asleep. He switches off the TV, which is playing on mute, removes the headphones from her ears, the glasses from her face. She murmurs but does not wake up.

The renovation is complete by late summer, by which time it is too hot, the porch—Jack's favorite part—uncomfortable to linger on for long. On Saul's last day of work, Jack gives him their news. An early retirement package and they have decided to move, not to the Keys as he had said but to Boston, to be nearer to their children and to their grandchildren.

"Leah is getting married to a Realtor in Amherst," Ellen tells Saul, as she deadheads a rose hip. "And Vivy has got a full-time job in Boston. She's expecting their fourth, a daughter. Everybody is there; there is no reason to stay here," she adds, musing about this and that as she moves on to trim the rose vine continuing its leisurely uninterrupted journey over the walls and fences that bound their property.

—

Saul isn't in town when Jack passes away. He has a heart attack while gardening. Anthony had been trying to help him push the wheelbarrow. The funeral is over by the time Saul returns and hears the news. He pulls into the driveway on a Sunday, a prearranged visit for a cup of tea and Ellen's jam tarts. He sits and listens while she talks. She has decided to stay. Vivy and Noah are moving back instead.

"They will stay here. It's a different house after all. There are rooms that Luke never knew; even the garden is changed. This is a house for children. It will be good to have little ones again. I do not blame her. And I cannot blame Noah. Luke went away, after all. What were they supposed to do?"

She does not mention Jack.

Saul wants to ask after Mary, but he does not. Instead he thinks about Jack. A sudden affinity seizes him. The way fathers are needed, and then aren't. The way women, mothers, take up the space of a home with their ministrations, the beauty of their innumerable acts, the ones without which a home grows gnarled and withered. But fathers like Jack, like himself, their steady presence so necessary to establishing the roots of such homes, when they leave, they go as if they have overstayed a welcome. Not missed. Not the way mothers are.

Ellen watches as he pulls away and waves at the last minute. She yells out to him to come back soon. He keeps her in sight in his rearview mirror as she picks up her mail, greets her neighbors out walking their dog. She grows smaller as she crosses the road, pauses to look at the house, then disappears inside. He chews on his wood chip as he drives, listening to canned faith on the radio. He has not told Ellen that he won't be around anymore. He is following his wife to Texas, where her family lives. Perhaps he will build a new house for them there. A place that does not contain the memories of how he and his wife drifted apart, quietly gave up on each other. He thinks this, even as he knows she is not a woman with whom renewal is possible. He will continue to wear white shirts, observe the disintegration of unions, the dissolution of relationships, participate in the construction of lives. Sometimes, rarely, he will bear witness to joy. He will create spaces to house these worlds. Some rich. Some poor. He will watch his children leave. He will hope for their return.

Kobe Loves Me

Rickey missed the bus because, well, he was unaccustomed to taking it now. He missed his ride of the past year and a half because he'd fought with Katie, who drove the blue jalopy whose doors could only be opened from the inside, and he'd pretended not to see as she drove by him, his best friend and her sisters crammed in the back as usual, having left the front passenger seat for him. If she slowed, he was sure she knew that he did not notice. He ran, then remembered he was not allowed to run, being male and tall and Black and therefore three times, perhaps six or twelve or more times, the problem, so he walked, then adopted a swagger since that was the way things had to be for everybody's sake, their expectations, his deliverance. He rounded the corner but at the last minute he swerved away from school. The students, every last one of them—the ones dropped off in SUVs at the front of the school, those being off-loaded on the sides and back of the school, the ones on bikes or hurrying to make the bell on foot because they fell within the walk zone— was hunched over. As if none of them were bundled up against the cold, even the ones in Orvis, REI, and Barbour. As if a communal depression had hit them. They were, despite their daily separations into the usual cliques—lax bros, stoners, hipsters, emo/goths,

meatheads, good-ats, et cetera—always, forever, united in this regard: basketball. They were Aces Nation. The school emptied to see
the team off on games in the middle of the day and that was allowed. The school was bused on taxpayer dollars to away games a
hundred miles away, even if the drivers had to be paid overtime, and
that, too, was considered money well spent.

Rickey had held the knowledge at bay overnight. Between his
mother's prayer circles that never ended because *God was always
watching*, his father being MIA, again, and his younger siblings
all needing food and help with homework, that had not been too
hard. They cared, they did, how could they not? But life was life,
and the here and the now needed attending. Last night, six-year-
old Booster had been running a fever of 102 and Rickey had been
chewed out by his mother for knocking on his neighbor's door and
asking Mrs. McGinty for help. According to his mother, white people were never actually helping. They were only *collecting informa-
tion*. Like that time when Bump got suspended in seventh grade
and all the parents who had been so generous and insistent on giving him rides and inviting him to birthdays and mitzvahs had
shown up in the principal's office to give statements. Well, not technically statements—they were expressing concern. Their concern
had made its impact, all right. That had been the turning point for
Bump. That was when he got all closed down and was never available to give Rickey a hand with Booster or Shy, never around to
get Milo off the bus. Nope. It was always Rickey's job. His job to
be the good brother, the good boyfriend, the good son, the good
surrogate father. Fuck it. He *was* the father. He was the man of
the house. *A solid Black guy*, Katie had joked along with him once,
though he wasn't Black. Not technically, according to his mother's
equations. *You aren't Black, Rickey. You can't be Black when your
mother is Filipina.* She said that even when he came home with a
hi-lo fade and a solid line to make the point. Said it as he applied lo-

tion to his knees and elbows. But Katie knew what he was; being a White girl gave you the radar for what constituted Black. *We should get you a cap with that embroidered on, babe! Like, #SBG!* They had laughed for a good while over that. It had been said on a drive to school and the whole car load had joined in. He'd have a line of swag with that on it. Caps, T-shirts, mugs. He'd become rich and known not for his rimshots but for being what he was. He almost smiled remembering this, then checked himself. At least he didn't have to be the good boyfriend now. He could be an asshole like every other boy in the school. At least that was one load off.

Yes, he had held it all in check until four in the morning when he woke up to get his own studying done. Numbers, of course, because the local news repeated it ad nauseam, like the date and year, March 23, 1996, the very day his older brother, Chris, had been born, when Kobe broke Wilt Chamberlain's southeastern Pennsylvania scoring record (2,833 to 2,252). How the team had ridden a thirty-game winning streak to that district title and their first state title in half a century, Kobe at the helm. Score? 48–43. Kobe, at fourteen, walking into the old gym. April 29, that same year when Kobe, the age Rickey was now, told a packed house that he was skipping college to *take my talent to the NBA.* They said he had worn sunglasses on his shaved head, and a sports coat with shoulder pads. They said he'd borrowed that from an LM line-backer for the occasion. Probably the last thing he'd had to borrow for the rest of his life. NBA All-Star MVP four times. NBA Finals MVP twice. Overall NBA MVP once. Overall points in his career? 33,643.

He'd seen the footage, run the plays, watched Kobe be Kobe, but he returned to different pictures. Kobe in the corner of the gym, his hat pulled down low the day before his Lakers games in Philly during Chris's time on the LM team—being watched by Kobe himself!—that newborn having grown up to be a player;

Kobe warming up on the Wells Fargo court, and Rickey and his whole family, even his parents together for a month, all decked in maroon, starstruck; Kobe's eyes watching him from the walls of the high school gym named for him. Those floor-to-ceiling images. Staggering. Like the man and his game. Most of all, visiting Kobe in California the previous year. The way Kobe had shaken his hand, given him a copy of his book. How it had felt to be standing next to him for the camera. The Big Ace, the little one, shoulder to shoulder. How Coach F's gaze had, for once, included him, Rickey, in the frame. What *that* had felt like, both hot and cold. Like something made large on account of his longing, but which had shrunk when he finally got it. Like he was smiling back, as required, but wished Coach F would turn away so he could go back to standing in that bigger light. Kobe's.

When Katie had called with the news right after it happened, he already knew. Everybody knew, it seemed, at the same moment. He had just walked back from the bathroom after a break at practice. He doesn't know how, but it seemed everyone stopped moving at the same time. Stopped picking up and dropping towels, shirts, stopped dribbling, stopped talking. Every phone rang. Only J answered. Their point guard, their star, already recruited to the Ivy League with a scholarship he didn't need. The way J's face transformed. The first name. The second, and a moment to register. Whom that second name belonged to in light of the first. Nope, he hadn't wanted to talk about it with her. Yeah, he was fine. He needed his brothers, he said.

"Your brothers?" That White Girl voice.

"Yeah, that's who I got to be with right now." And then, when she wouldn't stop talking, wouldn't stop saying he was hurt and posing, how he didn't have brothers on the team, he'd simply hung up.

The balls around them, motionless. The group of them, clumped together. One beginning, and then the rest. Doing what boys were only allowed to do in rage. At games. At games they'd lost by a hair's breadth. But not Rickey. He had just stood there. Just like he was standing now, rooted, not knowing where to go today. He took out his phone and checked the texts from Katie. Left them on read because he could. How that might come across, that, too, he could feel it. A hurt in his own chest. He checked Insta. One of Katie's friends had posted some #metoo bullshit. He shut off his phone. A Black hero dies along with his kid and there's a full-page article about some shit from seventeen years before. No eulogies. No respect for the dead, for his wife, his other daughters. Yep. Just another day in America. He shivered.

It had never quite reached the upper thirties as was predicted for January 26, and today, the Monday after, was especially bitter. He shivered again, then opened his LM windbreaker a little more, wanting to feel colder still. The skies were cloudy, the breeze like thin fingers feasting on raw skin. Snow intermittent and therefore unnerving. The chill had set in tight. Rickey hung back against the hedges of the McCoomb property that stood fairly adjacent to the school. The movement closed his jacket slightly and he let it stay that way. He could hear the second bell start. He'd still make it if he ran now. Still escape the detention that was never given to some of the other athletes, no point saying their names, whose children they were, what they looked like. What they ate, even. What someone else cooked for them. His stomach rumbled. If he didn't get in, there'd be no school lunch and he'd be even more hungry soon. He couldn't go home. Couldn't. There would be smears of pizza sauce on the wall from an early morning row; his father doing the throwing, his mother the praying, he and his siblings merely ducking as they got ready for school as though it was just the morning news on TV, things happening far away and not to them. His parents would be gone, but he'd still have to walk into that rancid air, that mess. At least if he stayed out, he could delay the work of cleaning all of it up, pushing the furniture back, wiping down the counter and sink just so his father or his mother—sometimes it was his mother who put God and his eternal need for prayers from the wretched aside and started in—could turn it all upside down again. Like he was a stagehand setting things up for the next performance. The image reminded him of the single theater production he'd been in because Katie had talked him into it: *Hairspray*. All that fuss just to put on a show that could include people like him. All the flack he caught from the team for spreading himself so thin. So thin that he could be even less of a baller than he was. That's what they said. Never mind that he'd never backed down from taking it to the hole for them, never hesitated to sacrifice himself for a Hack-a-Shaq, never said a word when he was left on the bench because some D1 coach was in the stands and Coach F had big plans for other players. Always for someone else.

Rickey swung back and forth a few times churning through flashes of memory, contemplating. In a scant few moments the decision was removed: the bell finished ringing. No school for him today. The crowd of photographers and journalists did not move. Nor did the cop cars. It was for the best anyway. He'd have had to sit there, Coach F going on and on and on about how he'd made Kobe and he'd have to chew on his lips and chew on his lips thinking Kobe was Kobe before you motherfucker, you just happened to be in the room with the title of coach when he got here. Kobe would have made twenty-one triple-doubles if he'd never played in your sight. And he'd be shaking his head and shaking his head and pretty soon Coach F would be at him for something like he knew what he was thinking.

He was doing it right then, Rickey was, shaking his head about all the goddamned shit in his life—sorry, Jesus, sorry, God—his mother's infernal prayers that he couldn't shake, that he found himself uttering like they had been carved into his tongue, his father's insatiable appetites that he had to constantly resist in himself, his younger brother's endless delinquency, the one temptation he never felt. Look at the two of them: he, already homecoming king, standing next to Katie, the most votes any king and queen had got in the history of the school, and there was Bump with an ankle bracelet for the rest of the year and dropped into remedial. If only Chris could come back from wherever he had fled to—he wouldn't say—Rickey wouldn't have to be the man of the house anymore. He wouldn't have to be SBG. He might actually have a chance to pull some shit of his own. Deserve the judgments for a change.

A cop car whirred briefly as though testing the sound of its own voice. Rickey shifted focus and considered a direction. Across the street he could go to the track, sit on the bleachers. He could take the back route and go to Suburban Square. Get a coffee. No money. Nix that. Not home. Not until he had to. He pulled out his phone and looked at another new text from Katie. The team was going to be part of a special assembly, she'd heard. J was going to lead it. Everyone was asking her where Rickey was. She was worried about him. Please text back. She'd be out in a beat if he asked her. She'd drive him somewhere or at least sit in the car with him. Like he'd done for her so often. Every fight with a girlfriend, every bout of feeling bad, he'd been there for her. He pushed that thought aside: her kindness would only get under his skin.

He took off down the road. Aimless now. He could feel the book in his bag. Kobe had signed it for him, written Rickey's whole name out, including his last name, Walker. Then he'd signed his own name, that shorthand illustrated with the I-own-everything flourish of a massive *K* and a *B* to match. The book had never left Rickey's possession. He hadn't read it, though. Never had the time. Couldn't read it now. The way Kobe's hand had felt on his shoulder just before he gave it to him. Rickey did it again. Shook his head. This fucked-up world. Of any flying thing that could come down from the skies, why'd it have to be this one? That was one greedy-ass vicious God.

We have lost our Ace. That's what the announcement from the school had said. Though who, exactly, was that *we*? Was he included? Nah. Katie was right: he had no brothers on that team. He was not good enough to be one of them. Didn't have *the right drive.* That's what Coach F kept saying to him. Kept yelling at him. Where did it come from? The right drive? The dedication? He didn't have no Jellybean in his corner, no father playing for the Golden State Warriors, the Sixers, or four teams in Italy. Kobe was born Kobe, but he was born to that father. Kobe was a young baby daddy at twenty-four, but that had been his choice. At seventeen, Rickey was supposed to give his all to the game but his all was also needed at home. And yes, his family was his, and he'd die for them, he would, but he hadn't made them. They hadn't been his choice, had they? He showed up every day at the court bringing everything he had. But everything he had was what was left over after he'd brought his all to his family. They couldn't afford to lose their toehold in the township, the golden ticket to safety two blocks from the place where he might blend in better, the very thing that had made his God-fearing mother move because when it came to what mattered, God was no help. No help at all. It was all up to one seventeen-year-old boy.

Nope. He didn't have the same drive as Kobe. Not even a distant close. Not even as much as the other not-Kobe-but-still-an-Ace boys on the team. Every last one of them going somewhere already. You could see it in their faces. They went home, they came to school, they played ball. Not him. He played ball and was father, cook, tutor, and nurse. Pre- or postgame parties? Not for him. Spirit dinners? He wasn't hosting. What might it have been like to be six, as Boomer now was, six, and in Italy? Or six and at basketball camp? Or six and at any camp anywhere? What might it be like to be fifteen and attending the same training camp Kobe had, as Rickey's teammates now did? Sixteen and not street smart but, instead, fluent in a foreign language? Seventeen and visiting Ivy League colleges? Getting help with his SAT prep? What might it be like to have discretionary income for recruitment videos? He hated that Katie was right. No brothers on the team. Nada. Rickey kept on walking.

His phone rang. Chris. A mostly one-sided conversation where Rickey listened yet again to his older brother recounting the glory days. He'd had them, for sure. He'd managed to be a real player in his time. A worthy Ace. An asset. *An Ace-t* as they put it. Chris had managed to hold on to their father long enough to make that happen. Chris had never had to bum a ride, or mount borrowed wheels two sizes too small, or risk a run down Montgomery to make it to practice or a home game. Coach F had looked Chris in the eye every time. Coach F had rarely benched Chris. Heck, that's how they'd all scored tickets to the Wells Fargo Center that time for Kobe's last "home" game. Chris had been talented and, most of all, undistracted. Chris had been, therefore, through no special effort of his, deserving. Rickey pursed his mouth and willed himself to keep the words he wanted to say trapped inside as he listened to his brother, glad that Chris had been lucky and resenting that luck at the same time.

Rickey had been nine the year Chris played for the winning team. Kobe had been teasing them for years for close but no cigars. Three straight losses to the Clippers, including at districts, and then the win.

"They'd won seventy-eight games straight. We were the underdogs. First day of spring break and the whole school showed up. I don't even know how many buses. All that distance. Nothing like it man. That kind of love."

He knew. Rickey did. About the love. He'd watched the school show up at every game leading to the final, watched them on the local news, performing an honor guard for the bus leaving for districts. Rickey had been there at the Giant Center in Hershey for the game that made them state champions. He'd watched from as close to the celebrated Dawg Pound as he could get, not yet in high school himself, but within throwing distance. He'd listened as all those kids, true to their tradition, finished the last four bars of the national anthem with spirit, drowning out the voice of some girl who couldn't hit the high notes. How shocked the opposing fans from Chester had been, the way other teams were at every game. Even now. *That* kind of psyching. He'd watched the game, watched the team, watched Chris, watched the fans. Those feet making drums out of the stands. Those cheers. *We believe that we will win. Aces Nation. Aces up. Aces fight.* The occasional jeer: *You let the whole team down.* The whole school, just like Chris said, crammed into a single ribboned section so as to make of themselves one, and therefore louder, bigger, more present than any row of flips the agile Black girls on the other side could manage to convey. They had stood throughout the entire game. The roar of those voices. And when it ended, when they won, the team had run, not to their families, not to the sidelines where Coach F was holding his hands in the air, jubilant, but heads first into the arms of their fans. Mostly Black bodies folding into mostly White arms. Held. Sixty-three to forty-seven after having lost the championship the previous year. But the real win was in that image frozen in his head.

"I'm late," he said, and hung up on Chris's *aight*, his head ringing with the sound of his brother's voice. His happy reminiscences had tightened around his own grief. Kobe had been their reason. Kobe had been their person. The one in their corner. A Black king who turned Black boys into princes with his eyes, his words, his tough. Rickey remembered that weight again. The muscled arm at rest around Rickey's shoulder, his own arms lowered, his fingers knitted together. A prayer of his own for his kind of god.

He looked at his phone before he put it away. They'd have dialed his parents by now, that automatic alert system, set in motion on account of some rich truant long ago, kicking into gear. No texts from either of them, though. He didn't expect any. They wouldn't be worried. They knew him too well. He was the good son. If he wasn't in school, he'd have an honorable reason not to be there. He reached the track.

On the opposite end, someone was standing. He squinted his eyes. An old woman. Older, he corrected himself, then added *lady*, thinking about his mother, how she insisted on respect. An older lady. No threat. He climbed up along the side of the bleacher, then sat right at the top where he could lean. The metal was cold under him. He stood up and emptied his backpack. Stacked his books beside him, *Mamba Mentality* on top, facedown. He folded the bag to use as a block between the metal and his bum, zipped his windbreaker, pulled his hat low over his head, and tucked his hands underneath his armpits. Across the way the older lady was swaying from side to side. He watched her. No, not swaying, she was stretching.

Rickey lay his head back and shut his eyes. He didn't notice the woman beginning her slow walk, the tip and correction of someone with bad hips, problem knees, other unseeable curtailments. If he had, he'd have known who it was out there. Mrs. S passed him by twice. It took her half an hour. On her third lap she stopped and rested on the bottom steps of the bleachers and finished her water. She wiped her face on the sleeve of her sweater and rose with great effort to her feet. She contemplated the track for a few moments, then sighed. She turned and climbed to where Rickey was lying, fast asleep, his mouth slightly open. He did not wake up until she sat down hard and heavy beside him.

He startled to sit and the stack of books beside him tumbled. He bent over and peered through the cracks. A textbook, facedown, and his wallet, contents scattered. His three-ringed binder, a spiral notebook, and Kobe's book remained.

"Good morning, Mrs. S. I . . . I got a free . . . " he said.

"I don't care, Rickey. Not today."

Her face was drenched and he wondered if she had been crying but then he noticed that sweat was dripping from behind her ears, which had turned red with the cold. Her thin brown hair was damp and chunked around her neck. He nodded, then shook his head. They sat there for a long time, staring out over the grounds. Rickey let himself relax. It was an unfamiliar feeling, being able to do that.

"He called me his muse," she said, and when she spoke, it was as though she was talking to a friend. "In his last interview here."

Rickey looked up. Mrs. S was crying. He folded his lips in, held himself steady. She continued to weep. He'd never taken a class with her. He was terrified of her. But he knew about that friendship. The stuff of confusion. And legend. Good enough for Kobe, good enough for him. He reached out his arm and patted her shoulder.

"He knew my reputation, but signed up for it anyway. Twice. As a sophomore he just wound up there. His English requirement. But then he took my elective too." Her voice was clearer now. "Twice. There are students who force their parents to make sure they don't get me. There are those who beg and plead with the counseling staff to have themselves moved out of my classes. There are those who stick with me once and hate me and then there are the ones who choose to come right back. He didn't just come back. He stayed." She paused. "He stayed in my life."

How perfect that the man that was only ever loved or hated sought out a teacher who had the same reputation. Someone was always bringing a complaint against Mrs. S, and someone was always singing her praises. Katie, for instance. How often had Katie cried at the different and higher standards being set for her? But then she'd get her papers back and it was like no other grade she received. What she earned from Mrs. S was a different kind of honor, more real somehow. He rearranged the picture. Set Katie aside, brought Kobe back into focus. Mrs. S talked on and Rickey listened. It was comforting. Unlike the emotions of the team. Unlike the way Coach F had bustled about readying a memorial. This was a quiet kind of sorrow. He understood it. Love for a man, his glory only a part of that. Maybe the walking had been an excuse. Maybe she couldn't stand the reporters and the school staff today either.

"He sent me a Radio Flyer wagon once, filled with baby stuff. For my new daughter. You know her."

Rickey nodded. "Yeah, yeah, she's friends with my, uh, with Katie."

"Love, Kobe." She scribbled the words in the air. "That's all the card said. Love, Kobe." She lowered her head again. Rickey felt the do-rag in his jacket pocket and considered it for a moment. It was for luck. He never wore it. It had been Chris's. He took it out and handed it to her. She raised her eyebrows, almost smiled, and waited, was he sure? He was. She took it. Blew her nose, a hard long sound in the cold empty morning. She folded it twice, then wiped her face.

"That's the beauty of life. You don't know how it's going to end," Rickey said, slowly, now looking at her. "That's what Kobe said, when he finished his interviews that day. The day you mentioned. His last game here in Philly. I don't remember it, but my brother—"

"Chris?"

"Yeah, Chris, that's what he told me today. I just spoke to him."

"How is he?"

Rickey shrugged. "He was good at the game."

They grew quiet again, alone and together in the silence. Mrs. S laid her own head back against the metal mesh behind the bleachers and turned her face up to the sky. The flesh on her round cheeks was streaked black and pink. At first he thought she was just talking but then he knew. Chris had printed the poem out after Mrs. S read it to the class. He had been a senior by then, when Kobe had sent his poem to his old teacher. Chris had pasted it to the underside of Rickey's top bunk bed where Chris could see it every day, and when he moved out, Rickey had in turn fallen asleep every night to it, woken up to it. He listened to Mrs. S now, the cadence of her deep, elegant voice issuing through that stern mouth. He repeated some lines after her, listened to others.

You asked for my hustle I gave you my heart
This season is all I have left to give you

He listened, and when she reached the end, Rickey said the last three lines with her. They said them slowly, delaying their arrival at the finish.

:05 seconds on the clock
Ball in my hands.
5 . . . 4 . . . 3 . . . 2 . . . 1

The wind gusted around them and they both hugged their bodies close. He picked up the book, still facedown, and flipped through it, reading fragments to himself.

There's something about being in a big arena when no one else is there.

Some people, after all, enjoy looking at a watch; others are happier figuring out how the watch works.

Gary was an Italian craftsman with tape.

He stared at the back of the book, weighed it in his hands, then turned it over. There he was. That tender profile, the eyes sated, gentle, a single bead of sweat. A life earned. Rickey let the tears come. For his afternoon in the sun with this man. His first time on a plane, a ticket paid for by Kobe. His first sight of the California coast. His feet in that water. Brought to him by Kobe. *Order anything down there*, he had said as the team left. *It's on me.* But Rickey hadn't left. He'd hung back for one more handshake and Kobe had tilted his head ever so slightly, smiled, and pulled him into an embrace. Father, brother, friend. For a second. For a lifetime. One Black man to another.

Mrs. S reached out and placed her hand on his. Her veins rose blue across her skin like lucky water. Thin, determined water snaking over a white and sunburned landscape, dry as his eyes would, one day, become.

The Irish Girl

I remember Madailein's first private words to me—their intimacy, their irreverence, how much they became her. "Jeyzus! Here I was telling the girls to be quiet! I thought you were praying. All quiet like a mouse." I remember that first voice, the way it blamed and loved me. "Why didn't you tell me, Don? Well, there isn't any point boozing by yourself, is there? You might as well join me."

And just like that we were kindred spirits.

Just like that I wanted to forget the hopeful purchase of new shirts and underwear from Bernard's, the red-edged fingers of the travel agent who guaranteed my flight in carbon-copied triplicate, imprinting the details with the manual computer that rang with such assurance at every line, even the holy water that the priest sprinkled on my grateful head. All those banal steps that brought me to Madailein, the minutiae of careful arrangements, all these flew up and resettled somewhere, elsewhere. Right then I knew it should have been something ordained. There should have been something impressive and inevitable about it. But there wasn't. It was merely a church thing. Wasn't everything back in Dublin then? 1969. A young father just waiting for his family to join him; that's what the Mother Superior had said to Mummy. Which wasn't wrong. But it wasn't the whole truth.

Mummy. Even I ended up calling her that in private, though she was barely older than me. Thirty-three years, one negligent and boorishly unoriginal husband named Henry, three daughters, and an ancestral home unlike any I'd ever seen. Hers was a labyrinthine network of small rooms. No central open space, the kind I was used to, no bordering sense to the movement of the household. Everything tight but for the women running through it like colored water.

"Can I call you Don, then?"

"Yes." She could hardly call me Don Carolis Appuhamilage Shyamlal Sirisena Perera, after all. "Yes, Mrs. Walker, that would be acceptable."

"All right. Don, these are my girls. Adele, Colette, Dedre. Fourteen, thirteen, eleven." She tapped each redhead in turn. "They are like their hair. The curled and difficult one, the straight and orderly one, the neither-here-nor-there one impossible to pin down. Girls, Don will be staying with us for two weeks as a boarder. You three can share your room during that time."

I said what I would have expected to hear from a guest: "I am honored to meet them. They are very nice children."

She startled me with her snort and the shove she gave the oldest one, the Curl, dismissing her protests.

"I will be quite comfortable on a couch, Mrs. Walker . . ." I tried again, inclining my head with just the right amount of deference, an ingratiating smile plastered on my face. Idiot. Idiot!

"Listen, Don. You want to stay here, you stay in a bedroom. I'm not having a half-naked brown man in the middle of my drawing room morning, noon, and night. Breakfast is at seven, dinner is at seven. The rest is up to you."

"Thank you, Mrs. Walker."

"Call me Madailein, for God's sake! Or Mad if you prefer." She laughed. A nicotine-and-chocolate laugh.

"Yes, Miss Mad . . . Madailein," I stammered, cursing my timidity.

I had felt so suave when I strode away from my family at Katunayake International Airport. Them behind the barricades, me in a three-piece suit and leather luggage with silver locks, a passport in one hand, free to walk in the restricted areas. And now here I was, stuttering over my words as though I'd never spoken the English language. As though I were any betel-chewing hired hand.

"Aah, you'll get used to it, Don. You'll get used to me. Dedre, show Don his room." And off I went with the Undecided Head skipping ahead of me, banging into this and that.

In my room I uncapped the leather flask that had once belonged to my great-grandfather. The governor himself had gifted it to him. His initials, EFK, engraved into the leather and filled with gold. A recognition of faithful servitude, I imagine. Our version of the family jewels after the governor left and the universities filled up with riffraff. No more English. Lucky for me that I had the nuns and fathers; the Catholic connection was my palanquin when I traveled. One call to Father Timothy O'Mahoney at All Hallows and here I was.

But still, I would have to tell her at some point. Father was not going to help me beg her favor. He had asked me to call myself into service. He had referred to me as his son when he said that. I soothed my sense of panic with a few blessedly flaming swigs from my pouch. There was no time to hide the bottle when the door swung open. There she stood, Madailein, like Botticelli's Venus, the hair lapping at her hips, herself all undulant cream, ripe.

She had hesitated to knock, she explained; a man of unknown national origin like him—who could tell what he might be up to? She had been raised in a Catholic country and gone to the nuns for finishing. She screamed as she said it, the voice trilling somewhere off to the right side of my head, a lark dying midsong.

"Finishing, Don! Can you believe it? Ah, I was finished, all right! I was done with the business of God entirely by the time I escaped. Do people do that where you come from? All the good girls go to finishing school back there?"

"Not exactly, no. They go to the convent."

"Leave it to the nuns. They certainly have it in for the rest of us women." And yet, silence, particularly behind a closed door, had always smacked of prayer to her. "I am so relieved to find you drinking whiskey," she said. She put her fingers with their serpentine ornate rings over her mouth in disbelief, not because she had interrupted me, but with delight at how things had turned out for her.

"Actually, I thought you were praying, Mrs. . . . Madailein," I said, "before dinner, you know."

We were both in God's country then, reveling in our own atheism, hedonism, even while we remained reverent and aware of the possible existence of piety. I told her that very night. My secret, the whole truth: when my family arrived, they would have to stay here with me. There was no other plan, no other accommodations from the church. They could only come if Madailein gave me permission to invite them, only if she decided that she could stand the imposition, the constantly shifting strain of hospitality toward foreign-born strangers. In short, I hoped not to have to leave Madailein's home after two weeks.

"If you can fit them in your bedroom, you can tell them to come," she said, one arm around my shoulder, her hand holding her drink, the fingers on the other one drawing calligraphy in the air with her cigarette. I knew even then that she was laughing at Henry and old Mrs. Mohrain, her own flesh and blood, who sat stern and unsmiling across from us at the dinner table, cutlery held just so as if they were mother and son united against the evil that had chanced upon them. Evil in the form of Madailein.

What could one do but love such a woman? What could I do but write and tell my wife to take her time, there was no hurry; this country was odd and I should get settled first.

—

Dublin came to me on two wings: one at work and quite another at Madailein's. I began my assignment at the Livermore Cheese Company learning, from nine to three each day, how to cure, process, and sell cheese. I was to go back someday and launch a cheese factory, a first for the island. But how could cheese compare to Madailein? I would watch the curds being separated from the whey and see only the cloudlike patterns on her scarves, the color of her skin. I would stare at the firming mounds thinking of how the undersides of her fingers looked when she pressed them to her lips to hide a smile, doing it backward, Madailein's way: the hard way, the wrong way.

The evenings and weekends rolled out at the Walker household, with Madailein conducting the troops, singing alone or to recorded music, playing on the piano in the front room whenever Henry went out. I basked in the chaotic grace of her ministrations, happy to be caught within the reach of her care. She hustled her daughters to their various engagements with military diligence, railing at her lot at every turn. She had so little time to be. No time at all some days to imprint herself on the world, forced out of discussions about politics and performance, withheld from opportunities to state opinions, be heard. Yes, something tightly squeezed into artificial beauty like the pink sugar roses my wife made with her cake-decorating set, not dripping clear and sweet and impossible like honey, a truer self. I set her free when I could—the children preferred staying home with me to sitting-in-the-car-with-Mummy—but not often enough.

"It is better if you just accept it, Madailein, then it doesn't seem so bad," I said one night, misguided. I was who I was then: young, male, far from my family. At first I thought she turned because of my voice. I had cultivated it carefully all day, practicing in the Livermore lavatory, speaking the words to the wrought iron trellises that bordered some of the houses on my walk home: the voice of an older man dispensing his advice. She was gathering herself together for another weekend of engagements entirely related to her children, but she walked over to me and looked me right in the eyes, her face half a bloom away from mine.

"Yes, like death, I suppose. That, too, gets easier if you just accept it, doesn't it, Don?" she said. I stared until she pulled a face and made me laugh. I would have kissed her then, and she would have let me, but I didn't know how. How did one kiss an Irish girl? I had read about them in a book I'd bought about Ireland. Among a list of Irish sayings was this one: You can't kiss an Irish girl unexpectedly. You can only kiss her sooner than she thought you would. Ah, how wanton they had seemed. And now here was one in the flesh, standing next to me. A real Irish girl. No, a real girl. And still I stood, arms at my side, at attention. Like a bloody soldier, all upright and, well, just right. Just right, just so, just nothing.

Nothing, yet surely something more than Henry.

Of course I hated Henry. He was worse than I could ever have been. He did not read or write or do anything really, anything worth talking about. He was just ordinary, and he turned inward like bowed legs and hunched backs and the fiddleheads on ferns I'd seen in my grandfather's botany texts. I wondered about women. Did he have another woman? It hardly seemed possible. Maybe it was the drinking that took him away. I didn't know why, when Madailein poured sherry like she did, like this was the first drink and the last. Who knows? Henry was sour. Smelled sour, talked sour. There they were, the damp, loamy earth of him, the airy bloom of her, nobody to pick her but me. And I, the fool, too timid to dare. Bold enough to laugh when she invited me to, but too lacking to know how to change her mood when she did not.

———

It was inevitable that she would do it: hand over her firstborn child to the nuns in her turn. To be overhauled with spurious, but determined, intent. Similarly, it seemed, the call from the police station was not entirely unexpected. She heard the officer say her name, state his precinct, and that was all she needed. This was her daughter, after all. The same blood, the same unspoken longings curdling her marrow, curling her hair. Colette—the Straight One—had run away, too, we found. Dedre spilled her sisters' story tearfully but with some defiance apparent in her jewel eyes.

"Col went to meet up with Adele so they could go out with the Dysart boys," she said. And the way she coated that word with her breath when she let it go! *Bhoyss*. As though they were inevitable and already on the march, riding dark stallions through the night. I wanted to ask Madailein to hurry, to rush to the girls and rescue them from those intrepid monsters, whoever they were. But I did not. I took my cues from her.

Henry was "unavailable" again, so I went with her and the youngest, a robe over her nightdress and instructed to remain in the car, to the police station. There she sat, Adele, feet barely touching the floor as she swung them, pursing her lips at the constable who had called the house. She wore a cardigan over her school uniform, and her hair was done up in a bun on top of her head. A grown-woman hairdo, with tendrils doing their best to remind us, and her, too, that she was a child.

"Colette's in the dustbin down the road, Mummy," Adele said, as we walked out. She was so pleased to say it, nodding her head like that, cherry-pout mouth, and swaying her hips too. Like her mother and nothing like her mother.

"The dustbin?! Why on earth would the child put herself in a fecking dustbin?" Madailein said, standing stock still, her hands on her hips.

"To hide, that's what," the Curl said, turning around and imitating her mother.

"Ha! Was the constable chasing both of you, then?"

Adele waited for Madailein's laughter to stop. She even waited for her mother to be done with wiping the tears from her eyes. Then she dealt her blow. "From you, Mummy. She was getting away from you."

She led us to Kevin Street, toward the rear end of Saint Patrick's Cathedral. Madailein said nothing. She didn't even slam the door to the car before or after collecting Colette, who climbed out of the dustbin with a frown on her face, angry that there was nothing to be angry about. Madailein drove silently up to the convent walls, the lights off and the engine in low gear, gliding to a stop. A surreptitious return in good faith of lost goods and, to my further amazement, whispered instructions on precisely how to climb the walls without sound. Not a single admonishment.

"Goodnight, Mummy . . ."

"Shhh!"

That was all.

I couldn't imagine why they left her, one by one. Those girls. She was not easy, of course. Unreliable, perhaps, now and again. But still. A mother like her, funny, present, beautiful, so full of life. I could not imagine why. On the way back she crooned a lullaby, and despite herself, Colette fell asleep. She sang in Gaelic and I did not understand.

I touched her with my tea. I gave her all my packages, with their red and green wrappings, their foil interiors, the bone-dry strength of the leaves inside, the aroma of it all. Beside the flask, there was nothing more precious for me to offer. I had brought them to give the priests at the seminary, but, oh, they weren't half as deserving, sitting in their stained-glass vaults, stiff as buildings themselves.

"I'll make it our way," I said, when she opened the first one.

"Okay, Don. You do that. I'll just sit here and watch you."

But she didn't sit and watch. She whipped around me transforming the kitchen into a stage set. A fresh tablecloth, flowers from the handkerchief of a garden behind her house, her best china ...

"Crumpets. Don, we need crumpets. I wish I could make them. Wish I knew how. That's one bit of domesticity they never got me into, you know, baking. I just don't know how to bake a bloody thing. Ah well, these biscuits will have to do."

Colette and Dedre were swept up by her enthusiasm. "Mummy, there's cake left over from Granny's birthday!"

"Let us have cake, then. But don't wake her. This is our tea party. Don, pour it out!"

No cup of tea, no piece of cake before or since could compare. There was enchantment in that cramped space, two crumb-ridden children, two tea-soused adults. Us four oddly washed up in a single-sunbeam-streaked kitchen down Liffey Boardwalk as if God himself was managing the lighting. She smiled when I said that, then gifted me with a passionately platonic embrace, her mouth on mine. The children made little-girl sounds of disgust.

"We're going to tell Daddy," Dedre said. "Won't we, Col?"

"Go ahead, then, my angels ... if you can find the bastard."

"Mummy was just being kind, Colette," I said, flushed and ashamed. Of her language, of my pleasure.

Madailein began to sing. "There's a hole in my heart, dear Henry, dear Henry, there's a hole in my heart, dear Henry, dear Henry, a hole . . . Come on, children! Sing with me!"

I sat while they danced around the table, hand in hand, the lyrics getting more outrageous with each revolution. Two blurs of blue and white chasing after the tall orange one, and their voices falling around me like the rain. What is singing but that singing? What is color but those colors?

"That's what we'll do, Don, we'll sell this tea," she said, collapsing onto the chair next to me, her hair undone and falling in great whirls down her back.

"I don't have enough tea to sell, Madailein."

"You don't have enough tea now, but you'll have enough when you go back home, won't you?"

We would become business partners. I would return home and send her crates of tea, tea by the shipload. She would sell the packets in Dublin and we would split the profits. It was a kind of entrepreneurship that appealed to the trader-caste blood that ran thick and strong through my veins, descending steadily from my ancestors as though we were all part of a single bountiful waterfall. I wrote home that night and told my wife of our plan. I imagined what we would do with all that foreign money. I would become a leading exporter. People would want to know me.

But the next morning Madailein said nothing more about the tea. Or the kiss. Henry was home and we all returned to sobriety.

~

It happened the night before the first weekend, when we were all scheduled to visit Adele at the convent, even Henry. I lay in my bed listening to the music coming from Madailein's room. There was no end to the music she played, or that she loved. From the recognizable strains of Strauss, to the compositions of Maksym Berezovsky, an obscurity even in his own time, she loved them all. I knew what she did in there, she had shown me, once: air-conducting an orchestra. Her musical talent was insufficiently satisfying: her voice, her piano, these things had no power to slake. In public she entertained us with her performances, her resonant voice, her artistry, but in private she dreamed of interpreting the music for thousands. For instruments she could not play, musicians she could not know, audiences she could not see.

The piece she was playing that night became my theme: my past, my future, running parallel to the dull music of the life I ended up living, struggling to win. It became the anchor to the exclamation mark that was my time with her. It became the full stop. The period. The end of every beginning. *Das Leben ein Tanz, oder Der Tanz ein Leben! Walzer op. 49.*

I was listening that night when, just as the music hovered over a held step, her imaginary wand trembling in pause, she screamed. I swear to this day that the house lifted and resettled, that I wet my bed, that the whole of Dublin itself, on both sides of the Liffey, forgot where it was.

Colette, Dedre, and I reached the hall outside the bedrooms together. Henry came out of Madailein's room. His mouth was turned down. There were no tears in his eyes, but I knew he was crying. Somewhere inside, in the places that men like him give in to sorrow, there was a gathering mound of ash. Whatever he had done to reach into her body and bring her still-beating heart out for such vulgar display, he had lost Madailein. The girls moved aside as he passed and then walked over to me. Did I know if Mummy was okay, they asked. Yes, she was, I said, go back to your room.

At dinner later, she declined the sherry that Henry brought out and asked me to serve, his own acknowledgment of guilt, his last appeal for forgiveness. It had to be bad when she declined sherry. Particularly when served on a silver tray. And by me. I did it with such flourish, she'd often said.

"Real silver, and polished to boot, Madailein," I said, pouring a second glass for myself as if to demonstrate the possibilities, attempting to lighten the funereal opaqueness that had descended upon us.

"No, Don. I do not want any sherry tonight." It wasn't unkindly said, which made it worse. As simply as that, the coordinates rearranged themselves to a time before the night of no sherry to every day after that. Nobody dared to ask for truth.

That was the end of it. Henry moved out and went to live on a boat by the quay, but she never played the piano again and, not too long after, I came home from the factory to find it gone. She stopped singing. Or at least, I never heard her voice again, that voice like things worth remembering, like old wine that has taken on the longing of the men and women who have gazed at it, waiting for it to age. Nothing could change her mind. Not even her daughters, all three pleading, uncharacteristically, in unison, could make her do it. And when the girls played her records, all the great masters seemed diminished somehow by her inattention.

A week after Henry left, she drove her mother to the nuns and left her to their fancy.

I remember that drive. How quiet we were, how much resentment and accusation and hurt hung in the burdened air. It was the only time I felt as if I was home, the way the two of them tussled silently with the power of what was left unsaid. It was a language I, too, knew how to speak. I missed my wife for the first time, and when we came back, I wrote to her and told her it was time for her to come. I imagined it would comfort me to have her there.

—

Sita came two weeks later, but she did not bring the children; she left them with her parents. It was her way of offering herself to me, her way of regaining control. I worked hard at Sita's behest, trying to finish my apprenticeship so we could return home quickly. I didn't mind, really; it was easy now that I was learning how to manage the rupees and cents end of things, not caressing the raw ingredients as though possessed, thinking incessantly of Madailein.

Those last few months I met Madailein only through my wife, with the stories she told when we stepped outside for a walk, or retired to our room after meals layered with tedious decorum. Mrs. Walker is a good landlady, Sita would say, more often than I could stand to hear the words. That was all Madailein was to Sita: a good landlady. I called her Madailein anyway, refusing to be polite, refusing to let my wife create formality and distance where I had experienced the full-bellied solace of desire.

"Maybe you'll come back, Don," was what she said when we left, bidding her our fussy farewells. I basked in her choice of words, the invitation that excluded my wife. Yet when I wrote to her, telling her the details of my life, I did not hear back. I wrote every few weeks at first, then less often and finally only once a year. A letter mailed with my idea of a tasteful Christmas card, the front decorated with the snows and fireplaces I'd never experienced, the ornate script inside wishful and quiet.

I did not send her tea in crates, or chests or even in a few loose bags.

Thirty-three years passed.

⁓

I do not know for what I have come, only that she has sent me a postcard.

*Don—The girls take turns caring for me. It's a sort of vigil for the
living, is how I look at it. I have grandchildren now. If you do not
have any family obligations, please visit.—Hurrahs, Mad.*

I am on my own and I stay at the new hotel, using American
Express like I had never known the feel of coins and colored money.
I do not stop at All Hallows, but I genuflect, haphazardly it may
seem to others, in the general direction of the factory.

The house has become smaller, the street has broadened. All the
fashionable apartments and still, still standing, the shrunken house
where I had, with the grace of God, chanced upon Madailein. I put
my suitcase down.

I stare at the door that I have pictured every day of my life. I ran
my palm over this wooden door when I touched my wife. I built
it into my own house and I held it open for my first grandchild. It
stayed shut in my dreams. And now, on this crowded street where I
am anonymous and enormously exposed, they are reabsorbed into
its solid strength. Everything that came after my few months behind this door goes back into the place outside it. The angle from
which I have viewed them: my wife, my work, my children. Between
the two there are three planks of wood.

The cuff of my long-sleeved shirt has disappeared into my suit
jacket. I tug it out and rearrange myself. People push past me, looking better and more purposeful than I had ever been. Even the iron
knocker seems to blame me for it, for Madailein, alone in all that
time. And me, too, now a widower, my children all grown, and
nothing more to work toward or look back upon but this lost moment, this startling, brief imprint of life. I wonder if she wears
orange still. Or perhaps she has aged into burgundy, distancing herself gracefully, outwardly, from the desires of her youth.

"Don!" she says, somewhere over my head, leaning out of the
drawing room windows. I wave. She blows me a kiss. "Come on up,

Don! The door is open!" I catch a flash of bright color as she ducks back inside.

No longer dressed in orange, but not exactly retiring in emerald green either.

Strange, now, to see how beautiful little Dedre has grown, how fully she takes up the space that her sisters once filled. The hair cut short and decidedly wavy, the high heels, the voice. Odd how such a woman withers in her mother's company, a second fiddle no matter how hard she tries. She is subdued, restrained, and only the subtlest inflections to her remarks indicate what lies within. A star turn, and it is not her. It is her older, less attractive, less stylish alter ego: Mummy.

"I went to the convent, but I was sent there for different reasons than the rest of them. She sent me because she wanted to get rid of me," Dedre says, her arm around Madailein, but her eyes sharp, airing her youngest-daughter grievance.

"I can see why!" I say, and we all laugh, creating our good old time, our fond memory. We all want to believe it. We all know it is not true. But we want it to be, aware of how close to the surface our own stories lie.

The tales are laid out again. It is all fine jewelry with few embellishments. Who needs them for this singular history? A mother, a daughter, an old friend, and the neighbors Madailein has called in to make up the numbers for a real party in my honor. I listen to the apologies, the reasoning, the thanks, the requests for forgiveness between Madailein and Dedre. I watch the extended hands seeming to stretch from one corner of the table to the other. Love, still, crouching behind every glance, skimming every intended cruelty.

When the sherry is served and I ask her, Dedre hisses in my ear. "No, it is certainly not Granny Mohrain's sherry service. That is at home, upstairs under my bed. Mummy would die if she knew Granny gave it to me and not to Adele." She laughs. The wild delight of outwitting her mother, of stealing what she had coveted for an oldest daughter, the daughter most like herself, Madailein squeezed in the middle as they both took their revenge—her mother, this daughter—for her lack of regard, her pursuit of some other pleasure, the way her choices had seemed to stack up against them both.

"It burns the soul, you see," Madailein is saying, "raising children when your mind is elsewhere. And yet, your body is . . ."

"Ensnared?" I offer, wiser now too.

"Yes! Ensnared, Don! Ensnared!" She slams her hands down upon her knees, sways forward slightly as if it has all been explained by the precise choice of words. She looks up again, the smile fading. Explained, but not excused.

Dedre clears away the dishes, and the table seems expectant and inappropriate without them. Nude, not naked. I am relieved when she brings out a fruitcake and some cheese and offers to pour coffee. She hands me a knife. It is Livermore cheese, and I stare at it, unable to slice.

"I'm buying a piano," Madailein says, cocking her head sideways at me as though asking for my approval. "I am ready."

I can see the orchestra again, there before me, and her with her back to the crowds, leading them to perfection. She is dusting off the remnants of a life, unfolding, fighting the untouched battle. I laugh, having been taught how not to cry in public. I want to reach out to her. I have learned how to kiss an Irish girl. But now I am too full of sadness. I understand this love, this half-life she has led, this guilt. The yearning that was once held constricted in a ritual of filthy backsides and grubby upturned faces and the relentlessly pitiful need of small people. Particularly daughters. And husbands.

"Adele will come on Wednesday, Mummy, and Col will be here for the weekend. Can you manage with Don till then?"

Madailein nods without looking at her daughter. "Dedre has to go back home to her husband and children," she explains to me, her reverent tone somehow managing to make it sound like a particularly inopportune and ridiculous crime to be tending to one's family.

"I brought you some tea," I say, taking it out of my bag, when she shows me where I will stay for the night. I take out the flask, too, and hold it out to her. "And this, in case you want to keep a little tot of something close to you for an emergency. Some sherry, perhaps?"

She leans against the door frame, resting her back against her palms. Her hair is coiled on her head and she reminds me of her oldest daughter: the same defiance, the same hair unraveling on her head, aiming for maturity and somehow falling short. Either I have grown taller, or we have grown toward each other.

"The English name for that piece of music is *Life is a Dance, or the Dance is a Life*," she says. "It always sounded like a question to me, not a statement. I was still figuring that one out when he interrupted me."

I bend down, carefully, and lay the brightly wrapped wooden box of six teas from the hill country on the ground. I put the worn leather flask, whose only distinction were those initials filled with gold, on top of it. She waits.

The Bridge

The right instant blesses and condemns us. For some people, it is on Fridays, because that is when parts become available, essentials like hearts, because of all the traffic accidents. It was a Friday when everything changed, but there was no accident. It changed because of Alex, who was going off to fight in a war I protested each Sunday afternoon on a bridge, most often alone, and because he didn't know that Sophie was pregnant. Sophie was my student and I did not know, until then, when she told me this news, that I loved her.

It's easy to love a student, any student. Just as easy as it is to loathe any one of them as I loathed David and Cameron and Justin among the boys, and all the girls except for Sophie. There was nothing to love about her, except that I wanted to be better than those who found nothing lovable in her. So I taught myself to pay attention to her. She sat in the front row, seeking safety through her proximity to her teachers, unavailable for the conversations that nobody invited her to join. She was middling. She didn't need special attention, nor were there sparks of brilliance to be found in anything she produced. It was as though she had been constructed of a particular sort of clay designed to avoid notice. And yet, here she was, pregnant, announcing to me that, yes, someone other than me had noticed her.

I had decided to sit through lunch in my classroom that afternoon. The staff lounge was unattractive even on the best of days, but on a miserable day when the snow is neither deep enough for cancellations nor clean enough for play, when it turns to slush by that no-man's hour between ten and eleven on a weekday morning, and there is only bitterness among the kids and resentment among the teachers, the staff lounge is to be avoided. I always sit alone anyway, unless Mrs. Nils comes out of her nursing station to join us teachers. Only she has continued to speak to me after the incident with the photographs. The principal had called me into her office to let me know that she did not think it appropriate that my class was exposed to images of the blood-soaked floors and scattered bodies of a prison with a foreign name.

These are not pertinent to the discussion of the trial, she had said. *In fact, I'm not sure that the trial is relevant to your lesson on American history.*

I had wanted to ask her if she even knew which trial I had been discussing, or request an explanation of how bringing those responsible for such crimes before a public court was not related to our discussion of the Nazi war trials, but I remained silent. I could not afford to lose this job. I could only afford to come to school each day, to have a routine, to be always only where I was supposed to be, and to make those hours count. And sometimes to take out those photographs and think about whether it mattered where it had happened, on whose soil such demons possessed a person. Or indeed whose soil was preferable when a war was required to be waged by men whose wealth relied on them.

And yet, in the staff room I had argued my case at the cost, it seemed, of my good name and the gradually established quality and value of my presence. Massacres on television, including on the nightly news, were grist for the mill, apparently, whereas photographs of naked brown men hung from prison walls or trembling in fear before fang-toothed dogs was *far too disturbing for eighth graders*. Not that I had many friends before then, but this was a good enough excuse for the acquaintances I'd made over seventeen years at the school.

Some evenings when I sat at home and stared at the family photographs on the mantel, those now long-gone memories of how life once had been for me, I thought about the people in the staff room, whether it was how I kept them at arm's length, relegating them to being no more than acquaintances, that made them so suspicious of me. *A man who has no friends*, someone once said, *is not to be trusted.* But had any of them ever been put to the test as I had been? Had any of them known, without any doubt, that they could not pass? Wasn't I better, then, than my colleagues who sat in judgment about my suspicious solitude? I believe so. I woke up each day knowing that I was not a good man. I put myself at risk all day long. Each night I went to bed knowing I had prevailed over my own evil. Another day when I have proved myself to be a good man. A good teacher. Kind.

I must not have heard her knock, because what came first was this: "Mr. Solmitz, it's Sophie. Sophie Laliberte."

Laliberte. She pronounced it *la liberty*. I always corrected her silently, and then recited the rest, *égalité, fraternité,* also in silence, after I called out her name during attendance. I wanted her to know that there was something out there bigger than her predicament, this gauntlet of slights and condescension and cruelties that she ran every day, every day, never one day of absence. I wanted to ask her why she came to school so relentlessly; I wanted to celebrate her fortitude and yet yearned for her liberation.

I waited, my daily bologna sandwich in hand. She waited, too, still standing by the doorway, until I rewrapped my lunch and put it away in its brown paper bag. That was something I despised: having to eat in front of people. It seems so uncivilized, now that I have not had to do it for over a decade.

"I am pregnant," she said. She approached my table and sat on the desk right in front of me, her legs hanging over, her eyes fixed on mine.

Watching her watching me, I knew I loved her and had expected something from her beyond her homework. Nothing romantic, nothing sexual. Just a commiseration of our respective miseries, our abandonment, our unspoken causes, any silent grievances and hurts we may have been unable to utter before. I didn't want her to be pregnant. Pregnancy meant things that were sticky, like cotton candy at a beach on a windy day, or like the fresh-shorn sheep's wool at the Common Ground Fair to which I had hoped, one day, to invite Sophie. Where she could have visited my booth, with its table of literature that I had put together myself, printed myself, paying for color copies, and passed out to the people who came to the fair looking for organic farm stands and handmade jewelry and who didn't want to hear about war or bombs or wiretapping or the fact that USA PATRIOT stood for Uniting and Strengthening America by Providing Appropriate Tools Required to Intercept and Obstruct Terrorism and had nothing to do with how they might feel about their fellow citizens or the country in which they had been born or were being asked to fight for.

I had wanted Sophie to see that I had things I did after school, and that the way the teachers treated me, or the way students disobeyed me, had not destroyed my sense of self, or my usefulness. I wanted her to realize that I fought hard for my goodness, to understand it wasn't easy for me in the face of what people put me through each day, but that long after the last school bell rang, I was still working, still standing. Whether in front of my booth at the fairgrounds, or in front of her in the classroom, I was victorious.

Perhaps I had wanted her to admire me for all that, to love me, too, a little in return for the example I set. A lesson that could teach her something useful for the conduct of her life. She could be truly grateful for it one day.

"I was married once," I said, caution set aside too quickly for me to stop myself and remember that she was a student, and there were confidences a teacher could never share with one of their number. Certainly not for someone with my past. I need not have worried. She was young. Young people admit only the most ordinary eventualities as being possible in the lives of the adults around them.

"Did she die?" she asked, unconcerned.

"No, she left me," I said. "We had children together. Two. We had two girls, Lily and Rose, but I don't see them now. They moved out of state."

"My baby will be born in September," she said. She looked down at a bag of chips she had in her hands, unopened, then looked up at me again as if she wanted me to explain the significance of the month, or to tell her whether this was a positive or a negative. "Alex Jared. That's the dad. I haven't told him. He's being redeployed. He's going back someplace out there."

She hadn't asked me why my wife left. I couldn't have told her if she had. I couldn't have said that when Julia Simmons was found beaten to death, and her husband with a bullet wound to his head not far from my house, everybody had assumed it was a murder-suicide, and nobody had thought to suspect me. I couldn't tell her that I, too, had fought in a war once and come home with no wounds except the one that made it impossible for me to be near a woman who looked a certain way: both frightened and full of hate. I couldn't tell her the way Julia had looked at me before I crushed her head in. How, at first, she had seemed grateful for my appearance when I overheard the rage-filled fight—the screams of *stop!* and *bitch* and *bastard*—on my run past her house and broke into the midst of their living room, and how she had crawled to safety when I came in the door. Before she looked at me that way, she had laughed, I was sure of it, when I pulled her husband off her, his fists flailing, the gun dropping from his hand and gathered by mine like a snatched toy. People who carry guns will always want to use them. They are like words that way. The nasty ones we think we'll never say aloud but always do when it can inflict the most damage. I wasn't thinking straight is just an excuse. What you do by reflex— that is who you are. That is who I was. I could not tell her that it had been the only time, or that nobody knew but me, and that this was the reason I had sent my wife and daughters away from me. This girl, Sophie, sixteen years old, she hadn't even been born when all of this happened.

For a few moments she was replaced by the boy she'd mentioned, the one who was going off to learn to do what I had done. "When does he, Alex, leave?" I asked, my voice as calm as I could make it.

"I was wondering if you would take me to Bangor on Sunday, Mr. Solmitz," she said.

"On Sunday—" I began, but she broke in, holding up the bag of chips as if in defense.

"I know you stand on the bridge on Sundays. I know. It's just that I've got nobody else I can tell. I thought maybe you wouldn't mind, missing one day, since you've been there since before it began and all, two years ago or whenever—"

"Four years ago," I correct her.

She's right, it would be just one Sunday missed, and maybe somebody else would show up the way they always do close to the anniversaries. One Sunday. But it would break my record of safety. Protesting the war was what got me started on getting better, feeling like I had never gone away. It was what made me feel as if I had a choice in saving the Alexes of the world. There are moments when I find myself stuck between wondering what would happen to my Sunday routine if the war were to end, and the realization that there will always be another war to add to my hand-painted banners. I want the wars to end but I need a reason to be counted among the peaceful. That bridge, it's my church. My weekly reckoning with God.

"I don't have anybody else to ask," she says again. "I want to write to him after he goes and tell him you're taking care of me until he gets back, with the baby, I mean. Helping me with the baby like an uncle. That's what I want him to think, afterward, you know, after he has gone. But I don't want to tell him now with him leaving so soon."

On Sunday I have to drive past the bridge to take her to the airport. The others are there, a handful of veterans like me, two whose sons are fighting this war, one whose daughter has died in it. A landmine, he said to me, though I never asked, and shuffled his feet. Each time I see him, I picture what it must have felt like to have strangers in ribboned uniforms show up at his door with a perfectly folded flag as though that would make up for her. Three who know that someone like us was responsible for how Julia died. Three who know it was me, and forgive me for it. I'd stayed silent each time the topic came up back then, among the others, civilians who had never gone to battle. When I shook my head at the news, they had nodded theirs, understanding. *Too bad about her,* they said, along with the others. *What he did to her before he killed himself.* Often one of them brought me an extra coffee back then, and patted me gently on the back as though I were the bereaved. It was one of them, Jim, who suggested that I send my family away.

"It's for the best. You know it. She won't understand, and she'll never forgive you, but at least this way you won't have to forgive yourself."

They took turns calling me up every weekend after Cecile left.

I couldn't get the image out of my head: Cecile in the front, Lily and Rose not even looking back once except for a quick wave; they were going to see their grandparents in Minnesota for the whole summer, something fun. It was not forever. In the end I mixed them together, Cecile, the girls, Julia. Alive, dead. Dead, alive. Until I convinced myself. I didn't need the reminders anymore after that. I simply woke up on Sundays and went to the bridge to be counted present among the living. To be accounted for, after yet another week of staying the course, as being innocent.

In the car beside me, Sophie is mostly quiet. She plays with the dial on my radio, bops her head to some beat in a song I can't place. I ask her the usual questions about family, futures, and she responds the usual way of people her age: upbeat, perfunctory.

She'd heard of the fair, she said. "My grandmother goes up there with some knitting group or something."

"She must be one of the craftspeople. There are quite a few. Very interesting folk. Bringing all kinds of crafts for sale."

"Yeah, yeah. They sell things. I think she said."

"You should come up sometime. With her, your grandmother, I mean. I have a booth—"

"Oh no. She says there are cows and horses there. Chickens, even. I couldn't stand that. I don't like the smell of farm animals."

"Well, it's quite large. The fair. There are whole sections far away from the animals."

"Yeah, she's asked me. But I'd never go. Not my thing. You know?"

She takes out a pack of gum and offers me a piece, pulled out halfway like a cigarette. It's almost glamorous, the gesture. I decline. I try to think of something else to say but my mind feels agitated between the beat of the radio and the snap of her gum. She rolls down the window, puts her arm out, and smiles at nobody, far away inside her own head. I drive on, wistful for my friends on the bridge. For solid ground. Next weekend seems far away, and the days between now and then interminable. I glance at Sophie again. The thin hair lifts off her ordinary face and pastes flat to her forehead. She looks so childlike. I have to remind myself of her condition, of why I have taken on this responsibility, of the fact that she is not a child but a woman. A young woman. Somewhere in this vast country one of my own daughters might have asked for a ride, been transported safely from one place to another. Maybe one of them has been in Sophie's predicament. I hope that someone decent came along to help them. Someone determined to do right by her. Someone like me, willing to put aside their own preoccupations long enough to show up when asked. When we park, I make sure to move quickly so I can open the door for Sophie.

Inside the airport we stand in the section reserved for family members. When the soldiers come in, she goes over to him. Alex. A lanky boy with dark, shorn hair and the turned-down mouth of a non-crier. There's a mother and a couple of brothers, but no father. When he sees Sophie, he looks surprised but then he shrugs at his family and introduces her. They nudge at each other like puppies and I remember this day in my life, the day my wife stood there and let me go, smiling, as if I were off to do something that required jocularity.

Somewhere they must have been playing music, because when the announcement for departure comes over the loudspeakers, it sounds like it has cut something else off. Alex turns into the embrace of his mother, who has begun to cry with the honesty of a mother. His brothers put their hands on his shoulders, participating, comforting, regretful, while Sophie stands and watches, that look on her face. The outsider who should be inside. The one who ought to be loved even more now for the future guaranteed, locked, safe inside her body. Nobody acknowledges it. Ordinary, mute Sophie, still invisible. I walk over and put my arms about her from behind, around her shoulders, resting over her chest, my cheek on her head. I feel her stiffen, then struggle against me, but I hold on. I hold on. Tighter and then even tighter, whispering *hush, hush.*

What Could Be Said about Pedris Road

Everything that happened could be traced back to brick and cement walls broken up by doors and windows. That's how she thought of the house in which she had grown up, a box in which she had been placed, along with her siblings—a cupboard more than a real house, with cutouts to let in light and people. There had been a landlord upstairs and a lower floor separated by a wall to make two flats rented illegally. Her family had occupied the smaller half. They had needed the address so her brothers could go to the right school. The one where all the politicians sent their children even if they didn't live within the right zone. That house, tiny in a way that nothing she saw on TV in this country, pursuant to the fad of minimalism, could ever match, its spaces inelegant and only serviceable to keep its inhabitants out of the streets, had been where happiness, or childhood, which were interchangeable to her, had been possible.

It was long ago, that time when she was much smaller, when the word *small* was the only one she knew to describe herself, other acculturations—exotic, petite—still beyond the horizon accessed by British Airways. She remembers now that first window. It was one of four that belonged to the flat, one of two that looked out from the single bedroom in which they all slept: she, her father, mother, brothers, and uncle. This window opened into a square of hard dirt the size of two saris cut in half and laid side by side. The two saris were her mother's. One was red and black, the other blue. Later, as she described the space with more sophisticated language, with terms that analyzed it for what it meant and not, as she had experienced it, for what it held, she explained that in concrete terms. Terms without the color and texture of saris: five feet by twelve feet. She corrected herself, no, six feet by ten feet, and then clarified it, small, like she had been.

"My mother had punished us, my brother and me," she told the woman now. The one who, when she stood up, was always shorter than she was in her high heels and therefore could not help her. Knowing that, if it were up to her, she would have refused to come to these appointments, but they had been ordered by the courts, executed by her husband. They were the only way she was permitted to be with her children. But she'd committed no crime beyond being unhappy in her husband's country. It made her angry, sometimes, sad, often, but they were natural impulses. Why was she being punished? Perhaps this woman would explain it to her.

"What had you done?"

"I don't remember."

"Why don't you remember?"

"I remember what we did there."

"What did you do?" the woman asked. Her name was large and older than she was: Margaret. Margaret Spelde. She wanted to suggest that the last name be extended somehow. To Speldewind perhaps. Something to balance it on a page. The way it was spoken now, it tilted to the left. Margaret had told her that her problems with left and right could be traced back to her inability to receive help.

"The left side is the receiving side, the right is the giving side. They say that people who are uncomfortable with the right being outweighed by the left are people who cannot accept help. They always want to do the giving. They want other people to owe them. They don't want to owe anybody anything."

Owe. A curious word. A sound that had meant yes in the language that was hers when she used to speak it, unlike now when she only referred to it as *the language of my country.* She had turned it about on her tongue wondering in which language it was being uttered there, inside her mouth, silently. *Owe. Owe.*

"What did you do there with your brother?" the woman asked her again. It was a question she had been asked frequently during the previous meetings, for her stories were always about her brothers, what they did together. At some point during each visit, there would be this moment of curiosity, the same question. As though playfulness, childishness, were incomprehensible. As though there had to have been something else going on, a deviation from a norm she could not, however much she tried, imagine. Her life back then had *been* the norm. It was this present that was deviant.

She summoned the gaze she had perfected, the one that she knew made her seem suspicious. It was her only form of control now. "We played."

"What did you play?"

There was a large flat stone there on the ground. She couldn't remember why that stone was there, clean and gray like it had a purpose. And then she did, because she remembered Mary. Mary was Tamil and Catholic and wore a bright orange sari like a Buddhist priest. She was fair skinned and she must have had curves because men had always whistled at her. She remembered that now, how the men had whistled at Mary and men only whistled at women with curves, not flat-chested ones like she had become. But she had circumnavigated that obstacle too. She felt proud of herself saying that word, *circumnavigated.* And then she remembered that if a person circumnavigates, that person would return to the place of origin. She felt crestfallen. A better word, then, something like *leap* but grander. *Leap* was a small word and she was no longer small. But no word would come to her. All the ones she could think of were small, too, words like *jump*.

"Circumvent!" she said, too loudly, startling herself.

"Was that the name of the game?" Margaret asked, pale, untroubled.

"No."

"We are talking about the game you played with your brother. Can you tell me about that time? What was the game? Why do you think it's important?"

"I circumvented the men," she said, stubbornly, pleased that she had circumvented the question Margaret had asked. She would out-last Margaret, too, just like all the others. She would make Margaret give up. She smiled. She knew the power of precise language. Her father had taught her that. Once, when she had related the whole story about how the neighbor behind her house had committed sui-cide and secured a last word in one fell swoop, waiting for his wife and toddler to come into the house and scream before kicking the chair out from beneath his feet, her father had said, *It's hanged, not hung. Paintings are hung. He hanged himself.* His life and its ending had become irrelevant with the correction. Only syntax mattered.

"Did the men play with you and your brother?"

"No, the men whistled at Mary."

"M-a-r-y." She said it slowly and wrote in her notebook. "Why do you think the men whistled at Mary?"

"Mary is real. Mary was real."

"Is there anybody who was not real?"

"Everybody was real. They are all real."

"Why would you mention this Mary just now? Did she play with you and your brother?"

"She worked in our flat. She slept in the kitchen, on the floor. She had a mat. She worked for us. She was a servant." Saying all this, she forgot where she was. In Margaret's place she saw the kitchen with its two-burner kerosene oil stove. She smelled the kerosene, the heady draw of it, how she inhaled whenever Mary had to refill the glass bottle, clean the wick, turn it over so it could do its work, that steady drip, the new flame. She saw Mary standing by it, a match in hand. How steady she was in all things. Mary shepherding her in or out of the front door. Mary staring out of the kitchen window in those last days before she left them. Windows, doors, windows, doors, Mary framed by each. But Margaret was asking questions again. So many questions about where she had come from, a life that resisted translation.

"Your family lived in a flat with one bedroom where everybody slept. And you had a servant?"

"Yes."

"You know that is hard for me to believe. You must tell me the truth. It is impossible to imagine that a family like yours, like you say yours was, forced into a one-room flat, could also pay for a servant. Was Mary a relative perhaps? An aunt?"

"No. I loved her, but she was a servant. She was very fair and beautiful."

"Fair? Did she make the rules, then? Was she a referee? Did she participate in your game?"

"What game?"

"The one with your brother."

She remembered, then, what she had been talking about. Remembered also what interested Margaret. That childhood, what terrible things might have scarred her such that she would be forced into this conversation. A new country was never responsible for breaking people like her. Certainly not this country. This was the dream country. She was the ungrateful nightmare, refusing to stay fixed. Look how hard they were trying, her husband, Margaret, even now.

"So how was she fair?"

"She was fair. In her skin. She was fair skinned. Light skinned."

"Oh." Margaret smiled faintly the way she always did. She wanted to fault Margaret for this somehow, to assess a lack against her, but she couldn't. Margaret was fair, heart fair, not skin fair: Margaret had not been enlisted to beam at her; she had been enlisted to find out with questions like her next. "Did you like Mary?"

"I loved her. She bought us Cracker Jack chocolates when she got paid, and naarang bik when she wasn't paid. She chewed betel with hunu, so her voice always had a bubbling sound to it, from the spit in her mouth. She could spit in a hard stream and sometimes it looked like she was bleeding from her mouth except that she was controlling the bleeding, putting it out and pulling it in whenever she pleased."

She stood up to demonstrate. "She tilted over like this when she spat into the drains, gazing into the places where the red spit was landing as though she was painting a picture and wanted to make sure."

She sat down again, feeling lonely without something more to say about Mary. The room she was in was very foreign. Everything was foreign and unusual. The lamps and the shades and the carpets, not a room with a single bulb, curtains, and cement floors. No open drains.

"What made you think about Mary?"

"She never went home."

"Why didn't she go home?"

"She didn't go. She wanted to stay with us. My mother teased her. When Raheema's became a big store . . . it used to be a small one, a kadé, with a few things to sell, kadju, seeni kooru . . . sorry, peanut brittle, sugar . . . sugar sticks, sweets like that in big glass bottles . . ."

She faded away wondering how she could explain the differences to Margaret. How Raheema's had gone from being a little store to a big one, how precisely this bigness was defined. What could Margaret know of the difference between Bristol cigarettes for rich men and beedis for poor ones? Could Margaret picture what a hairnet fixed to a round cardboard circle might look like, or its purpose? What about the packets of Sunsilk shampoo for fifty cents? Fifty cents in the currency of her country, not this one, which belonged to Margaret. Or how the proprietor, Mr. Raheem—though of course she had never called him that, he was just a shop owner, not a gentleman—had secured the adjacent lot and wanted to expand his store. How could she explain to Margaret that her parents, who lived in a one-room flat, were still important enough to be invited to an opening ceremony by a shop owner? How could she explain why the opening of a shop was an event at all? Such things were heralded through market predictions in this country, and celebrations were associated with organic grocery stores, the kinds of things that changed a housing market. Not small convenience stores like those in her own country. She stared at Margaret, and tried again.

"When the shop opened, my father was away, so my mother didn't want to go. She sent Mary." And into the frame came the precise anecdote that had reminded her of how her mother teased Mary. "She sent Mary, but she put her hairpiece—my mother had a long hairpiece that she tucked under her own hair before she rolled it into a bun. It made her bun enormous. I don't know why she used it. Her own hair was enough. And the hairpiece sometimes stuck out, so her bun had different colors in it. It would have been much better if she didn't have that hairpiece."

Why did her mother use a hairpiece? It interfered with the shape of her face. If she hadn't had a hairpiece, if she hadn't tied her hair into a bun and covered it with a hairnet, everything taut and tucked except for the strands that she scraped loose with the edge of her comb across the two sides of her middle part, would her father have stayed with her? Her father had called those pieces ang once.

Ang. The horns on cattle. She had stared at her mother's head. Her mother had been taller than she was then, and still powerful. They had always seemed important to her, those loose strands of hair. And suddenly they had seemed stupid. When had she lost her own eyes and taken on those of her father? She was always replacing her eyes with other eyes. Her mother's. Her father's. Her mother's. Her father's. Back and forth, back and forth until nightfall. Until she shut her lids and put back her own eyes and could not sleep. Until she got on a plane and slowly worked those eyes out of her own, scraping and peeling and worrying until she was here, in this room, looking with her own eyes.

"You were talking about Mary," Margaret said. "You're frowning. What happened with Mary and the store?"

"My mother's hairpiece had two strands of short ribbon at the top of it; that is how she tied it onto her own hair. She called Mary and told her she had to go to the grand opening on my mother's behalf, and when she was ready, she pretended to arrange her sari. Mary wore it like a lungi during the day and only put the fall over her shoulder if she was going out. My mother slipped that hairpiece into the waistband behind. It looked like a tail. Then she sent her to the store."

"What did you think of that?"

"I laughed," she said, and laughed again, remembering. "Mary came back and scolded my mother and told her how all the men in the store had teased her. She said my mother was like a child. My mother laughed till the tears came. Mary laughed too. It was a happy day. We still talk about it sometimes. The time that Mary went to the store with a tail."

"What happened to Mary?"

"She went home. She was sent home. My mother said she had

a fruit in her stomach. A growth is what she meant. But we were small and we imagined a large round fruit. She said Mary had to go home to have it removed and then she would come back."

"Did you believe your parents? Did you never question them about what actually might have happened to Mary? For instance, did you not think she might have been pregnant?"

She shrugged. It had not occurred to her that there had been anything but illness to explain Mary's departure. She resented Margaret for suggesting that she should have questioned her parents. That was not something you did back in her country. It was civilized that way. And in any case, those had been the sweetest days of her life, those days when her mother played pranks, when all she had to do was go to the Montessori school nearby that her mother's friend ran, play with her brothers, and be looked after by Mary. That most of all.

"By the time Mary returned, we had moved from Pedris Road, where we didn't have a number on our door, to a new place. A real house. But she didn't want to stay."

"Why do you think she didn't want to stay in the new house?"

She shrugged. "Maybe she was pregnant," she said at last. "Maybe she never had the abortion she had been asked to have. Maybe my mother couldn't let her stay. After that." It was the truth, she could feel it in her bones. She could feel her resentment of Margaret growing stronger. She shrugged again. "I don't remember her much in the new house."

"Did you miss her?"

Of course she had missed Mary. But what was there to do about it when her mother so often went to school with bruises on her body, and her brothers stayed out late, and the only company she had were the other servants who came to stay for a while. Each had been sent away after a few months. Only the ugly and aged lasted. She had made friends of each one of them.

"My mother read *Everybody's Book of Fate and Fortune* to ask if Mary would ever return. She said Winston Churchill consulted that book before every decision. She borrowed it from a friend who belonged to the British Council. It was very large. I had to stand to look in it. She made dashes and dots on a piece of paper and then found the answers."

"What did it say?"

"My mother always wanted Mary to come back. She was her friend, even more than a servant. She trusted her."

Would things have been different if Mary had come back? Would Mary have stopped all the other doors and windows from opening or closing or having to be locked or gazed at or frightening her? Would it have helped her feel less terrified in this country that she had come to of her own volition, where every child was always in such peril, particularly her own? She might have learned to be sweet like Mary had been, learned how to manage people differently. Instead all she had was fear and anger, her sharp words, and her wit. All she had was a succession of what her husband called incidents. Knives under her bed. Lurking outside the school gates long after her children had been dropped off. Periods of silence and then the rage. If only Mary had returned. She would be sweet. She would not be in this room.

"Why do you think you talked about Mary?"

She looked at Margaret for a long moment, trying to muster up the courage to tell her everything in a way that would, perhaps, help her understand. But that would mean betrayal. And she'd already left her family behind. She played a different card. One that favored the linear storytelling Margaret's country liked.

"Mary washed our clothes." Margaret was silent, nodding, waiting. "Mary washed our clothes on the big flat gray rock she kept in the area outside the bathroom. That's why it was there. She carried it into the bathroom when she washed clothes. She put it next to the basin and then she beat the clothes on it. The basin was white enamel."

She remembered that basin. When they were very small, her mother bathed all the children by holding them across her lap with their heads hanging over the basin. When her brother was old enough to panic at being held that way, out of control, naked, his head lower than his body, she stopped. They all stopped together, even though she and her other brother had been squirming over this ritual for a long time before. It couldn't stop until her oldest brother had had enough of it. The firstborn. The second born. The last.

"My oldest brother wasn't punished."

"I see. We have come back to that story. Good, good. Tell me why you think he wasn't punished."

"I only remember that he wasn't punished. I don't remember what we had done to be punished. My mother shoved us into that square of space and she shut the bathroom door. That was the only way to get there. The square was surrounded by walls. On one wall was the entrance to our bathroom. On the second was a window from the kitchen to the flat next door. On the third, a window from our kitchen, where Mary stood and watched us. On the last, the window to our bedroom."

After the door shut, she and her brother had explored the brown earth, a place they never played in, preferring by far the long, narrow parapet approach to their home, the flat bars of steel that had been brought in to build a bigger house and abandoned in the overgrowing grass beyond it, the white farm gate beyond that, things they liked to swing on. That gate had shut once, leaving them inside alone, and what their mother had said as she left had come true: the steel bar they had been standing on, she, her brothers, and the neighbor's boys and girl, had fallen on this brother's foot and fractured it for a hard cast. A few years later he had got hepatitis A and lain there for months, yellow eyed and weak, eating only seer fish cooked white and rice, drinking powdered milk in a yellow plastic mug with Marie biscuits, food bought just for him. The neighbor had once screamed her way into their bathroom with a gagging daughter, and their mother had placed her mouth over the child's nose and mouth and sucked out wads of phlegm that she spat on the floor, large gelatinous yellow pods of mucous, and brought her back to life.

She remembered now how her mother had managed to throw a birthday party for her when she was five and had won a blue watering can in a school race when she came second and she had to yell the correct pronunciation of her name into the microphone next to the nuns. She had watered her mother's potted plants that cluttered up the front of their house bordered by more walls and a wall for their feet, too, where her father pulled out their four chairs, so close for lack of room, and drank with his friends, who were all homosexuals, and slept in their beds, if they were too drunk to go home. Once she had walked into the kitchen and seen Mary on her back with her orange sari above her waist. Her father had discovered it, the fruit that sent her home. Another time, her mother had made warm tapioca and the table pushed against the wall to make room for one pink desk and one blue desk for her brothers and for her to share had seemed like it had expanded, the heat from the pudding wafting up, the teaspoons her mother had taken out of the blue chest that had come from Rome—along with her father, returning after six months service there after being dispatched by the government, carrying household goods, dinner sets, and cutlery—set beside each small bowl. She had felt like a dormouse. Small and safe and cozy at a table beside their last window, some sun coming through, themselves clean, and one-time tapioca pudding on the table. Cozy. Once.

But that day, she and her brother had examined the dirt in the small square and this is what he had said: "Let's play a game so that when they come to the window, we won't look sad. We will look like we're having fun."

He had thought up the game: they collected ants from the dark earth and placed them on the clean, smooth rock and watched them crawl about looking for something. They had only picked the black ants, the harmless kind who traveled fast and in a state of seemingly inebriated chaos, not the red ones who went about in single file and bit brown skin into welts.

Their mother and her oldest brother had finally come to the bedroom window. Their mother had pointed to them, her and her other brother, as though to show him where they were, to reassure him that they had not disappeared. Her mother had stood there toweling his head dry, powdering him, and putting Johnson's Baby Eau de Cologne behind his ears, under his armpits, and bending down, out of sight, to rub it between each toe. And he had looked sad behind those bars; his head tilted like he did not understand, his wise eyes solemn, his mouth soft, his hair wet, his arms hanging from his shoulders. That is what she remembered. That scene. Those words from her brother about what to do, words that had seemed like the only way to survive, nothing ever to be told of, or shown, as it actually was, only something else.

"What happened?" Margaret asked, her whole body waiting.

"Nothing," she said, her hands folded quiet in her lap. Her lap of blue jeans, its pool of white cotton blouse.

"Nothing?"

Yes, nothing.

Margaret gave up after a year of stories about windows and walls and parents and siblings she would not name, and the silence in between the thoughts she shared. She wrote *citalopram* on a sheet after six months, *aripiprazole* after nine. Their last meeting was conducted in silence. Margaret asked no questions; she kept her voices inside, repeating two words to herself, *Marge Spelde, Marge Spelde,* to correct the imbalance. She said the name to herself long after her sessions had ended.

She was not forgiven. Her punishment was made permanent. And given the choice, to stay outside and never see her children again, or to be contained and have them visit under supervision, she chose the latter. They placed her in a small room, a room within a building, a single window looking into a courtyard where other people walked. They sent her home.

Matthew's Story

I was the firstborn and, for a few lonely years, an only child. Then we were two brothers. We were four. We were three for a while, but it was the wrong configuration. If one of us had to stay with the twins, James and Jude, if it had to be three, it should have been he, not I, who stayed. One day they will talk about us again as one, Gabriel and me, inseparable again, as we had been from the day he was born. This was the thought that crossed my mind as I lay, still, waiting for the morning and what it would bring. It is what allowed me to get dressed in a white shirt and pressed khaki pants. They are the clothes of mourning. They will be the clothes they bury me in.

—

I follow the woman in a blue dress. The blue of my dead brother's eyes.

She has come early, walking up the long driveway, her eyes cast down. She does not seek the faces of the other visitors scattered, petallike, around her. She does not pause by the guest book. She walks through the house. I watch the color as she moves. Stopping before a photograph, she meets my brother for the first time. He has been reduced to a single moment in a hurried frame, blown up so that the distribution of pixels is as much a work of art as his face, angled into the lines of laughter.

He will not turn twenty-four today. He will not be married today. This is only our first day without him. Her dark fingers touch my brother's likeness and the sun of the afternoon overtakes her and me.

"Matthew, move over! I want to get a picture of Gabriel alone." My mother's voice, rising and falling across the open field.

"But I want Matt in the picture, Mom." He holds on to my hand.

"We'll take another one with your brother, Gabriel. I just like the way the light picks up the colors in your hair."

It did. The light. The way it never could reflect off my black head, the way the light is swallowed by the black of my eyes. Gabriel is tilting his head in the picture. There is sunlight streaming behind him, the rays straight and visible as if he had been delivered to us by a munificent sky. The back of his hair is golden, the front in shadow. His chin is lifted in defiance: that was a first for him, and I loved him for finding a way to put me into my mother's photograph. I remember how I smiled, then aged as my mother turned to me, her face closed; it was a small price to pay for my brother's gift of inclusion.

The woman's dress is long, the neckline high, the blue fabric a smooth and liquid peace that I want to touch. I rub my fingers together involuntarily.

She stops by the basket of envelopes. Some are cards, some charitable donations to a freshly discovered cause, a new purpose that came into being with the treasonous nighttime curve of a back-of-hand familiar, cherished road. Her dress brushes the old sideboard. My father made that, his hands covered with the kiss of fresh pine from our land, his eyes limpid the way they got when he worked with wood. We played in the trail of sawdust our father left between the kitchen door and the back porch. My brother and I. Us.

She stands by herself in the room without purpose off the kitchen and sips from a clear plastic cup full of warm cider, long black hair falling in a nunlike veil around her face. Nobody notices her. A still, blue story. Her at her window, and me outside, where I go to lift my eyes skyward to the clear day and the sound of trees in the wind. The mountains hold on in the distance and there are no clouds to blur the lines of our home. The roof is sharp, solid, mirroring the steep descent into the valley beyond. I see the once-possible future: grandchildren walking up the slope to the orchard that my brother loves, their parents, themselves barely grown, behind. My mother laughing, my father too. I see myself watching them from afar.

Someone approaches me. I do not want to turn my head and become available. I do not want touch, one hand extended, the other resting on my shoulder. Always the right shoulder. My brother was left-handed. Last night he flung his arm around me. Last night I had teased him, my baby brother, always the baby, no matter that the twins came after. *Tomorrow you get married*, I hear the words I'd said, *and from tomorrow you are Maggie's to mind*. It was only a wedding present that I had wanted to give us, just one chance for him to be foolish and reckless like me. *Let's trade places for once. You be the bad boy, I'll be Gabriel.* I wanted to stand by and admire his devilry. The way he had watched me all my life.

When I turn toward the man beside me, I see that it is one of my father's old friends. I walk outside with him at my side. We stand by the rock wall bordering our driveway and I listen to his regrets. His left eye pulls down slightly farther than his right and there's a scar through his eyebrow. Perhaps he had an accident. Maybe in his younger days. Sports, perhaps? Football? He has big hands. He must have looked handsome with that injury. Some girl cheering from the stands, Coke in a sexy glass bottle in her fist, bobbed hair, some girl fainting in horror when he fell. Where is she now?

"Matthew, is there anything we can do for your family?" he offers, his hand insistent on my right arm now. He is slack lipped. Perhaps they didn't get married after all, he and that girl. Maybe his friend took her home after the game that night, and maybe the friend looked too whole and perfect and present and she forgot her boyfriend. So whom did he marry, this old man? "Do you need any food afterward? Or any arrangements for the memorial service? There will be a service, won't there? In a week or so?" he asks, staring at me now.

"I'm not sure—"

"Well, of course, but if you think of anything, anything at all, let us know."

"I will," I say, and still he waits. He starts to shake his head and I am certain that he will begin to talk about losses he has experienced, and surely he has had many, his hair so gray. Maybe that girl's name was something like Delilah or Lisa and he will start talking about her. How she came back to him and how she died too young in his arms after thirty-nine years of marriage. "Thanks," I add quickly.

"Okay, son, okay. Take care of your mother. She's a lovely person. Just a wonderful woman. And your younger brothers too. Take care of them."

"Why?" the word escapes from me and hits the man.

"Just take care of them," he says, frowning a little. "It's your job."

I say nothing and he lets his hand fall away from my shoulder. He looks at his hands and I see not his hands but my father's, the way he had stepped into the room where my mother was lying, tired from the rehearsal dinner, her feet up on two pillows. The way he had stood in the doorway, his shirt and palms covered with my brother's blood. Her quiet question: *Which one?*

"Laura!" The woman he hails is compact and attractive in the usual sort of way. She looks up at the sound of his voice. Laura. Well, close enough. He goes to her without another word. I watch how he puts his arm around her, sheltering her, as if there were something coming after them. But I do not follow.

I stare after them in the left-behind quiet. I erase the red on my father's white button-down dress-up shirt. I think of the woman in blue. She is not among the people I can see from where I stand. No longer by the window. I start to go in to look for her, but my mother comes out. I step over the rock wall and walk backward toward the first trees. My mother stands uncertainly on the doorstep. She has risen, as has always been her habit, to the occasion. She wears faded jeans and a close-fitting black shirt, crisp, ironed. She is beautiful, full of grace, even now. Alone in a sudden lull, she seems lost, my mother who knows only how to comfort, how to give, how to receive need, keep safe. A woman who had always thought it was too good to last, though I know the answer my father gave her was the one she feared most to hear. She does not see me and I back farther to stand behind the trees now. As if invisibility can protect me from my mother's eyes and from them, these strangers I will never see again, their curiosity about our lives, our elegant grief.

I see my brother now, standing beside my mother. He hugs her, his breath warmed by the Moët & Chandon that he sipped repeatedly, flute after sweet flute with each ribald rehearsal-dinner toast. I refused to make one, though he begged. *I'll get you tomorrow, brother. Brace thyself.* That's what I said. He is pointing to the sky. He is warm, demonstrative. He says what I cannot, does what I never learned to do, is light within the darkness that I bring. My mother smiles; she kisses him and pushes his hair off his face. She has to reach up to do this. He is tall. Taller even than I am.

It is late, but the moon is full. I sit on the rock wall waiting for him. I am home for his last hurrah and this is enough for him, something to celebrate, to memorialize with some shared caper. It is

our way. It has always been our way. Ever since he turned two and I
held his hand and helped him walk the circumference of the raised
well at the bottom of our father's land.

Someone greets my mother and it is daylight again. There is no
moon, and I am not sitting on the wall waiting for him. I am behind the trees. Hiding.

After my mother leaves, I slip into the house to search for the
woman, looking for the forbidden color she has brought into the
house, something small, yet larger than her slight frame. My refuge.
She is leaning against the side of the back deck, gazing at the view. If
I can keep her in my sight, I will make it to the end of this day.

I walk past her and up onto the low ridge behind the house. I
see our land through her eyes, the stark, solid, that's-enough-of-that
beauty of central Maine, the idyllic setting loved into being by my
father's ancestors. How it must have appealed to a young carpenter
with a new wife. My mother, lithe and full of longing. My father,
like me, awkward and so in love, the children coming in unplanned
succession: me first, my brother next, the twins six years after. My
mother blooming among her thorns, all of us men adoring her in
our own way, mine perhaps the least known.

I see him running for the first time up the hillside to where I
stand now: my brother on the fleeting short legs of toddlerhood.
He giggles, stumbles, falls, looks up at me from the grass. I laugh
at him, refuse to help him up. *You can do it! C'mon! You can do it!
Stand up. Like this.* I show him how. Lie down, leap up, walk ahead.
He struggles to keep up with me. I am three years older. I know
how. I am proud of the things I can teach him.

The blue fabric rises in the breeze and she folds her arms across her
chest, holding on to the warmth of her own body. She presses closer

to the wood behind her. The wind presses the color of her dress into the deck like spilled paint.

Blue eyes turn brown when they are shut. He is all brown as he lies sleeping, naked but for the shorts he wears, touched by the sun of an outdoor summer. He is twelve. I nudge him awake, a finger to my lips. Long lashes open. In the flashlit dark, I see them: the blue of the cornflowers, of the sweet new berries on the fringe fields of this haphazard land we call home. A living color that he carries carelessly on his face. He puts on the clothes I hand him and follows me down a staircase we have learned to keep quiet. We are outside, cold. We stumble past the fruit trees, letting the fragrances cling to our jackets, eat through the fleece lining, anoint our still-warm bodies. He goes where I go, not needing to know why I must or why I choose these paths: ruts over grass, rocks over paving, over the mountain never around it, unable to take things as they are, unwilling to let go of choice.

I came first, I go first. He follows.

We walk through the night and he says nothing, able to trust me, not knowing that it is his faith that makes me brave. When I stop, he raises his eyes to mine, waiting for instruction. It is not enough that the deep indigo skin stretched overhead is pierced all over with stars, or that he can hear the relentless sound of the water flow, fall, and meet the rocks below in a single movement. We both hear the wild call of an owl on his wing, and still he stands, looking up at me, waiting for the invitation, to be told my rules. I shrug off my jacket and he understands. He shakes his head, shivering in the cold, small bumps sprouting on each surface that he exposes. I am already at the water's edge. I take his hand and we step in together. I feel the tight squeeze of narrow fingers clutching mine as we hesitate for a moment, waiting for the numbness to take hold. Then we are submerged, swimming along the bank to the place where the water grows silent before the fall.

I see his eyes, widened by the moon, shadowed by the night. Terrified. He follows me down to the rocks below, letting me guide his feet, showing him safe places on the sharp edges of the descent as we climb down. An eternity with the water around us, on our heads, in our eyes, mouths, cold bodies moving within a cold tomb. We stagger out at the bottom and I can't tell if the wetness on his face is from his tears or what we have just conquered. His smile comes to me on a moonbeam, warms me, warms the salt in my own eyes, dissolves it. I take his hand again and again as we climb up the slope, dodging dry branches, hanging on to the roots of trees planted by our grandfather. When we reach the top, we are sweating. I help him with his jacket. I hold him safe beneath my arm. We walk home together, never having spoken a word.

The woman in blue is standing where we had stood that night before we went in, at the side door at the back of the house, the place where we found my mother waiting for us, no secret in the world ever wholly hidden from her. That ancient intuition.

She says nothing, my mother. She holds out her arms and my brother folds into her, everything that I gave him gone, the heat of my body lost as he is consumed by the fire of my mother's love, her eyes burning with the never-asked, never-answered question as she leads him indoors, almost shuts the door. I stand and watch the halved light. It seems to utter a conditional welcome I cannot abide. I turn and face the mountains again, think of the passionate sting of freezing water. I can imagine it: the return to water, as before, wading in, a swim and then no climb, just a single leap. It is the thought of my brother finding my body that roots me there.

A long while later I hear his voice floating prayerlike from the window above me. A whisper: *Matthew! Are you there? Come on*

up. Hey, Matt? It's all right. Mom's gone to bed. I go inside, and let
the stairs creak, not caring whom I offend. I go only because he has
called me in.

There are others arriving and I see the woman glance up at the sky
and then at the flash of silver on her wrist. She presses her fingers
to her eyes, lowers her head. I see the tiredness creep slowly along
her body as she curves her shoulders inward, a flower fading out of
reach of the sun. A door slams and she jerks upright, steps forward
away from the house and into the light. The blue pours forth again,
diminishes her, raises him up, makes me stumble in my stride. She
goes inside.

I move quickly through the thickening stream of visitors, trying
to catch up. My head bent low, eyes averted, I charge between them,
walking down the slope and back to the house. It keeps them from
approaching me, even those who do not know enough, yet, to lay
the blame on my deserving head.

Maggie stops me.

"Matthew, could you brew another pot of coffee?"

"Sure," I say and start toward the kitchen, but she pulls me back
by the sleeve of my shirt. She looks at me with such kindness, this
almost sister.

"Are you okay?"

Am I okay? This was to be their wedding day. In the foyer there
is a large serving dish with a pen that writes on glazed pottery.
People dressed in gowns from Marty's and rented tuxedos were supposed to have signed their names on it while a band played country music in the background. That's what Gabriel loved: country
music. Maggie didn't, though. What were they going to play? I
don't remember now. Only a few facts have strayed to the surface
of my mind.

That the serving dish is covered with condolences.

That there are wedding favors stacked by the door for our visitors to take with them when they leave.

And that in the next room are all the platters of hors d'oeuvres rerouted for delivery to our home, where they wait like pretty flower girls, so colorful and so edible that nobody has touched them.

But mostly that serving dish with its grand size and delicate edges, the vine pattern along the handles. Where did Maggie plan to store this iteration of their hope? Whom would she serve off it now? What?

"Maggie," I start, but then I stop. She waits for me to say something, do something. To stroke her cheek perhaps, or ask her for a favor. She continues to look at me, her face tilted as if for a kiss, hopeful. "Maggie," I say again.

"It's okay, Matt, I'm okay," she says, lowering her head, nodding, and then falls forward into my body. I put my arms around my brother's love. His love since he was thirteen years old. She wipes her face on my sleeve and rests for a few moments against me and then she cries some more. She cries until everybody has heard it or of it, and of my dry, unrepentant face, too, perhaps. My mother comes in. Maggie passes from my arms to hers. From stone to warm clay.

"We need more coffee," I say to my mother. "Someone needs to make more coffee."

"Go make some coffee, Matthew," she says, her tone soft.

I shake my head, then leave her and go upstairs as if I had been interrupted in an errand, as if there is anything worth needing now. I pass the bathroom so I use it. I hear footsteps on the landing outside: the twins, trying to find a quiet room to smoke. I come out and motion with my head toward Gabe's bedroom: nobody has gone in there but me, and it is my lot to give them permission to encroach, to defame it even if only with their own unoriginal insurrection against our home. They acknowledge me with a joint declaration from their tawny heads as we cross on the narrow passage that has connected all our nightly trespasses; my parents unnaturally adoring of each other, the twins in their world, Gabe and me in ours, linked by a closet whose crawlway we never shut even in adolescence. No, not even when we had to, simply had to put our hands down our pants.

I press my back to the wall to let them pass. We stop moving for a short moment. It is almost an embrace. We turn our faces away, all three of us, unable to make it last, unable to say anything more. Gabe took up my heart and I had no room left for these younger siblings; I had nothing left to give after him. What words should I use now? Now that there is nothing between us?

I feel dizzy as I stand at the top of the staircase looking down at the crowd below. She is suddenly visible again, among the others, right in the middle of the room. The center of a flower where only the center has meaning.

He was not first, would never be. What did he want of me? Or I of him? Nothing, surely. And yet, and yet, that untapped joy within him. I wanted it to pour forth. I wanted it to bear me. A stream along which I would not have to swim, a fall that would still hold me up, weightless till it placed me upon the foaming rocks below, everything turned to a bright red flame, the dark ice gone. Oh, to be worthy of that! My midnight journeys, the lost days of my youth, battering the iron carapace of winter with my pickaxes, looking for fish I bloodied and returned to the deep lake waters, the speed of the trucks I grew up to drive, all the girls and women I would never bring home to my mother, all of them worth something. To be adored. Not because I had come before him but because I had given my life for him. Existing in the half he would not visit, cavorting in the wilderness of my own making, wooing the things he could not understand. All for him, keeping him safe. My life a movie he could watch from afar, enjoy, criticize if he must, but never join, not really.

How could I have grown tired of my charge? When did I decide to end my stewardship?

I wanted us for one night to be two people, not halves. I had wanted to be him.

Blue. Blue. Blue. One color that weaves through the shades of gray and black, the hues of mourning. A way for people to die just a little bit, draw less attention to life. And the absence of it. Why has she worn blue? She who has surely never beheld the brilliance of his eyes? She is searching for someone. My mother lingers beside her briefly, familiar as though they are friends. They move away and are gone from my sight. The room is empty once again. I climb down carefully. I resist the temptation to sit down and rest my head against the wall.

I sweep the pictures and paraphernalia into the drawer below the sideboard and the display is done. The construction of a life for anonymous sorrow seekers. We owe them nothing, my brother and I. I want to shoo them out. Fruit flies! Maggots! I cannot breathe. Someone helps me outside. I hear their voices, low, comfortable, generous in their non-lost world. I shake off the hand at my elbow, stride away with purpose, make it to the crest of the hill, turn the corner, and catch the branch of the first apple tree in my brother's orchard before my legs give way.

The grass below me is still green. Newly mown. I smell the fresh scent of my labor as I watch him walk over to me, his feet dancing from the drink. Out of the home-lit warmth, the embrace of my mother, and forward into the dark. His body alert, his eyes awash with a keen-sensed thrill, the anticipation of something new. The me-too delight of a second son. For a few moments he is shorter than I am on the slope, and I smile and ruffle the hair I had just seen my mother smooth back over his forehead. He clasps his hands together.

"Ready?"

"Yeah, I'm ready. Mom says I should rest for tomorrow, Maggie too. But tonight's my last night, right? Last night to cut loose." He hugs himself and shivers. A childish grin. He sways a little. He is two again. He is eight. He is twelve . . . fifteen . . . sixteen . . . eighteen . . . he is twenty. He is waiting for me to show him how I live. He is almost twenty-four.

I stand up and he follows me to where I have left it. The machine looms up suddenly. I know it scares him, but he feigns confidence. Just like me. I watch him assess his skill against the uneven construction of the vehicle. A stupid invention, driving over terrain that we should feel with our feet, trapping us with its noise where we should run in silence. How solid it is beside him, this lanky, skinny brother of mine. I swallow. Panic rises within me and I feel a sudden urge to stop him, but the feeling is overcome by the slap of his palm against the brute vehicle and it is as if it and I are being egged on.

"Ready?" I ask again, though I know both answers. The right one and the wrong.

"So . . . ?" I listen to his questions. My overview is quick. To keep it light, make is seem manageable, give him the kind of confidence you need to master the things that can kill you.

"It isn't that hard," I tell him, "as long as you keep it steady."

His eyes meet mine over the wheel and we both smile, a familiar giddiness enveloping us, bringing us together again. Then, he is gone, the lights illuminating the road ahead, leaving me behind with the night. The roar of that engine. How it stuns our laughter into silence in its wake.

It fills my head. I open my eyes wide to watch him go but I do not see him. I am shorn of all memory, naked in the light of day. A firm hand touches my forearm. On my left. She stands before me. The blue intensity fills my head. Her voice is deep. Her eyes stay level with mine. She touches me as if she knows me, stays, though I offer her no respite from the task of comforting those who refuse to be comforted. *Kill yourself a brother first*, I have said, wordlessly, to all who came near. And only she has heard. She tells me her name. Nothing more. Her eyes do not leave my face, nor mine hers. We stand there in silence. *This blue*, I want to say, *this blue is . . .*

But she has turned away. I watch her go. Her dress catches on the rosebushes by the fence. She bends down to yank it free and it tears. She winces and she brings her fingers to her mouth. I see the swift, sure ooze of living blood, taste it on my mouth pressed against his. *Breathe! Gabe! Breathe for me!* I shake my head, run to catch up but someone calls her name and she leaves me behind. I crouch beside the bush and remove the piece of blue from the thorns: just as much as could be held in two eyes.

When I stand up again, I see her walking away from the house, her step as steady as when she came. I start toward her. My mother stops me to ask if I have seen my father, to stroke my cheek, to smooth my hair. I linger in this transplanted act of love. Over my mother's shoulder I see her car move out of the line of others still parked, still waiting for a pretimed end to ritual. The rutted road slows her and the car dips and climbs around the first bend. I turn my back on my mother and try to follow her, run, nearly catch up. She reaches the second bend at the same time as I do.

This is as far as I can go.

My steps slow down; her car speeds up.

I dare not turn my head.

I smell the already decaying flowers and the fresh blooms neatly laid by anonymous hands. Someone, a neighbor perhaps, has filled in the skid marks. There is no trace of him. But I see him. I am still and I am running away from our house, toward the sound of things ending, toward crushed metal and wheels going nowhere, toward myself, my brother, my life. I hold him in my arms, his crooked, all-wrong body and my mangled soul clinging to each other through heaving breaths and the howling madness of my voice raging at the night. He has no face. I taste the blood in my mouth.

Gabe. O Gabriel. My angel.

I fall to my knees. I press the shredded blue into my eyes but it is not enough. Somewhere farther along the road I hear her car come to a stop. The door slams. I stay down. When she kneels beside me, I see it, clear: less than a year from now, I will drive too fast down this same road in an ordinary pickup truck. She will attend that funeral, too, but this time, she will wear black. Gabriel and I will watch her together.

I lift my eyes to hers in gratitude.

First Son

What I remember first are the fingers. My aunt is holding the door shut, and she is crying. On the other side, my uncle is crying too. But it is he who holds the kitchen knife. And it is my aunt's fingers, visible only up to the first knuckles, that stay on my mind.

They were fighting about property. Every fight was about ownership and birthright, claims to which we, Buddhists, are never supposed to consecrate ourselves, certainly not at the moment of death, though we are practiced at lingering: blown about as gray ash, tossed into rivers, spread among fields, tipped off the edge of a precipice. We are expected to leave everything behind except our sins and our merits, which will decide our next incarnation. Instead, we drag our mourners with us when we go, causing them to look up from weeping only to take receipt of ancestral feuds, to possess and possess the land.

The funeral, at least, had ended. My grandfather was now gone, taking with him anything that could be asked for or given: regret, forgiveness. Nothing remained but pieces of paper and an unwieldy expanse of land farmed by tenants known only to my grandmother, now eighty-one; my father, the secretly favored son-in-law; and the second of my two older brothers, the best beloved. There was no animosity between those three, no. All the grief, all the rage belonged to the daughters, especially my aunt, who had married a low caste, and my uncle, the oldest son, whose side-shuffle gait and now-pout-now-grin mouth were but the visible manifestations of the lacks he had carried into the world at birth in his own two hands. Two hands with weak artistic fingers unable to play anything but a simple flute, the bata nalaava, and even that with only two notes, known to us children and ridiculed by the adults, as twa-twa.

"Asoka, stop that twa-twa!" my mother would yell and my brothers and I knew from an early age that the world contained some wickedness we would become intimate with one day. We could tell by the way his face crumpled and only the pout remained, his eyes cast down under an easily summoned frown.

Which is why when he asked, his voice trembling and his hands shaking, if we would wash his shirts, we would do it without a word. Even me, the youngest, at the age of eight. The feel of that hand on the backs of our heads paid in spades for the drudgery of getting the grease off the collars of the shirts he wore to the job his oldest sister's husband, our father, had arranged for him to inhabit for more than a quarter century: welder. This scion of a high-caste landed proprietor and a princess of the ruling elite, this sibling of an engineer, a bank manager, a teacher of Western classics and English literature, and two women of leisure, worked as a welder at a small business near our home. He was paid a pretend salary of 150 rupees a month when he began, 350 by the time he retired thirty-five or so years later, and went from boardinghouse to boardinghouse because of the arguments.

The arguments were usually on payday, when he got drunk and spoke of his heritage. Nobody believed his stories of grandparents who owned tuskers and had a multitude of servants, of being driven to school as a boy in laundered white clothes, of the one brother and four sisters who lived in the city, of his nieces and nephews, including one at an American university called Harvard, which, he told them, was the best in the world. Above all else, nobody believed the story of his piece of rice-producing, coconut-tree-lined land.

But it did belong to him, this piece of land. His father had ensured that, in this respect at least, he would be treated no differently than his siblings; he would get an equal measurement of land. Except that his plot of land was the least cared for; it had the lowest yield, and it sat across the road that divided the contiguous estate from the smaller lot on the other side. *In case it was sold,* they said to one another, *in case he gambles it away when he plays cards and drinks kasippu with the union organizers who live in the park.*

For us children, that land was made of myth and fairy tale because it contained an island.

The year my grandfather passed away was the last year we visited that island. During the coconut plucking that our grandparents attended, driving up from their pillared, veranda-decked walauwwa to supervise the hired hands *who could never be trusted,* we kids were set free with just a few cautionary words.

"Be careful when you are near the pluckers!"

"Watch for snakes!"

"Don't go too far!"

The watcher's wife was sent periodically to check on us. She would provide us with kurumba from the young coconut trees, the clear water sweet and cool in our mouths, the flesh inside scooped from the spoon-shaped device she carved out of the husk. She gave us pieces of sea salt, one hand cupping the other with due respect, to ease the sourness of the raw mangoes she peeled and sliced at our request. Her own children stood guard, fingers in their mouths, bright curiosity in their unblinking eyes as they watched us from behind her body.

To reach the island, we had to jump off the road and take one of the ridges that checkered the fields. That was another difference: the land this uncle owned had no wide access way, with planks laid on supporting beams buried into the moatlike river that irrigated the fields on either side of the road, no gate posts or padlocks, no watcher to be summoned with the beep of a horn. His land lacked any barbed wire. It was open to all beings that populated heaven and earth. My brothers and I believed that there were more serpents and crocodiles and birds around and in his fields than in any other place, for surely it appeared to them as it did to us: mysterious, welcoming, fragile.

That last visit was also the only one we made with this uncle, our Loku Māma, a titular respect bestowed upon him in recognition of his birth order and his role as our mother's younger brother. The title had no corresponding material goods by which to buttress it: no car, no advanced degrees, no ability to bequeath anything on us but his presence. I don't remember how he happened to be there. He had never accompanied us before. Had he been on leave from his job? Or was he "on probation," as he often was? A trick also arranged between my father and his friend, *to manage Asoka*, and used whenever the latter issued a drunken threat or created a scene at a family do. This time, unlike all the other times when we had ventured across the road to the island, we did not charge ahead, our thoughts on getting from the road to the island without disturbing something venomous or sharp toothed. This time, we strolled.

"This, putha, is my land," he said. We stood on the road, waiting for the right moment to leap down. None of us said we already knew. "This is what your Aththa has set aside for me." He patted his chest a few times and we watched, three faces turned upward. I remember us that day, so young, my older brothers just eleven and ten years old.

"Putha," he continued, including me, and I smiled back, accustomed as I was to un-gendered status among my retinue of brothers and male cousins, "someday all this will be mine. When my father is gone, there will be nobody for your Loku Māma. But I will have this."

We gazed at the fields that glistened under the morning sun, new rice brightly green against the muddy brown earth below. Around us the day was still, only the small sounds of fast-flying insects and the screech of the occasional group of black crows above our heads. A breeze sang over the rice and made us all flap our clothing to catch it; my brothers lifted their shirts up to their armpits and I tugged at the front of my dress. Something splashed in the underwater close to our ridge and we moved to the center of our perch.

Beside us, Loku Māma was silent. His mouth turned down, at the thought of that bereft future or at some current lack, and his eyes welled up as they did often, usually before a full-blown attack of weeping, but just as regularly before a violent lashing out against whichever sibling or parent or brother-in-law had the misfortune to be close. The only people he did not fight with were we three children and his younger brother's wife. The wife of the brother he despised for being normal, for his achievements. I wondered why many times, over the years. I imagined that in her presence he remembered that he could have had such a wife, had fate not touched him with his shortcomings. After all, we knew that to be true and we were only children. Loku Māma had great love and great kindness. The type that children sense instinctively and trust forever. Which is why we continued to stand, waiting for him to decide which it was going to be: sadness or rage.

"Let's go, putha. I will show you the rest, but you have to be careful. There are snakes here. You have to watch where you are going."

Unlike all the other adults, it was my hand he held. The youngest, the girl, still a girl despite the seemingly seething masses of boys swirling about me, inside and outside the family, coming at us in yearly streams from the all-boys schools at which my mother taught and my brothers and cousins attended. But not for Loku Māma. Like my grandfather, he referred to me as the Damsel and predicted great fortune for me in the future. A future full of learning, and accomplishments that would change the order of the universe. The kinds of predictions designed to win the heart of a child and, also, to direct its future.

"Where is the Damsel?" my grandfather was given to inquiring, usually of my grandmother. If I was within earshot, I would pause to listen to the accolades I knew would follow.

"Your Damsel is out there climbing olive trees and mango trees higher even than the boys!"

"That's okay. Damsels must also have fun."

"Like a monkey! Not like a damsel!"

"I should give her a little more money now for reading the newspapers to me."

"How come there is no money for the boys?"

"She reads better than them."

And into the lack of response that followed this I would walk, basking in my favored status. My grandfather would be sitting there, stroking the few gray hairs left over his exposed skull, chuckling at my grandmother's pursed lips. But these are memories carefully resurrected as an adult. As a child it was merely the way things were.

The difference with Loku Māma was that I noted every favor I received from him, even as a child, accepting it with care, enjoying it then as much as in the afterward of looking back. Like that day, his hand holding mine, helping me to walk through the fields, even though in truth it was my hand that steadied him as he tried to take care of me and also keep an eye on my brothers. It was an excess of simultaneous responsibility that was hard for him to manage, wired as he was to take in only a single stimulus at a time.

Up ahead of us, my brothers' feet had gained speed. Loku Māma quickened his pace. I matched my step to his, trying to stay ahead of him, knowing that if we were too far apart and I yanked back, he would slide right into one of the bordering fields, and he would be blamed for whatever mud we got on ourselves attempting to rescue him.

"Putha! Avindra! Stop! Don't go too fast, Putha," he gasped, equally fatigued by the heat as well as his panic. "I have to be close by." He let me go for a moment and clapped his hands together several times, to get their attention. "Mahinda, Putha, wait for us. Nangi can't walk that fast. She's small!"

Of course my brothers would not listen. They knew better. But so did I. "I'll tell," I shouted. That was all that was needed; their pace slowed until they came to a halt. We caught up with them. One of them cuffed my head, but they allowed Loku Māma first, then me, to squeeze by, sideways, so we were now officially leading the foray. Ahead of us loomed Ovitiya—a generic name, we children learned much later, given to any such landmass in the middle of a field of paddy. Back then we assumed it had been chosen in consultation with astrologers and with great care, the name uttered in an auspicious time by the head priest at our great-grandfather's temple or someone even before then. To us, longevity and enduring ancestry appeared to be the true measure of worth.

"Wait!" Loku Māma said, his palm held up like a traffic policeman's. "I will go and see that everything is okay and then I will help you up."

We waved our heads vaguely, side to side, in agreement, and shuffled in place. What could there be to harm us, after all? Securing an all clear was an adult preoccupation. We were willing to stand aside and let him venture forth and return with the satisfaction of feeling more capable than we were.

Loku Māma tried to climb up onto the raised earth by holding on to stray plants. The plants he picked were the wrong kind, the transitional type, with shallow roots and deceptive leaves, hardy in appearance but brittle.

"Try the other one, no, not that one. The other one. That big one in the clump!" my oldest brother yelled. Such moments always appear to require yelling.

"Take this," the other brother said, giving him a sturdy dried-up branch of coconut flowers that he had picked up along the way. "You can push this into the ground and then with the other hand you can grab the top." These further instructions were taken by our uncle, whose comments were now self-deprecating, on account of his incompetence, now full of curses at the shabby earth itself and all the equally shabby plants that had landed upon it.

"I must get the watcher to put up a proper set of steps here," he panted, talking mostly to himself. "That rotter does no work all day. He should cut down a couple of coconut trees and build a nice bridge to go up here. Then you, my little ones, won't have to worry about falling off this. It's very dangerous. You must only come here with your Loku Māma. Otherwise you must stay on the other side next to your grandparents. You hear me? This is not a place for small children. Not a place for you. Putha? Avindra? Mahinda? Both of you must never let your little Nangi come this way alone."

"Aththa won't let you cut coconut trees," my second older brother said, matter-of-fact. This was the brother who never learned to varnish the truth, who grew up to believe that truth was the way to varnish the blows of life.

Loku Māma had reached the top by now. He looked deranged in that moment; his hair, usually slicked down with Brylcreem, was sticking out to the right side of his head, sweat was streaming from his hairline, and there were large stains under the armpits of his red short-sleeved shirt—the same shirt he always got dhobi-washed for *good occasions* where decency was called for. He laughed, and his grin, which we ordinarily found delightful in its uncontrolled generosity, was now more a grimace of crooked betel-stained teeth held in place by cracked lips. "Your Aththa . . . your Aththa . . ." He stopped to catch his breath and step. He made a sweep of the fields behind us with one arm stretching out from the seemingly cavernous interior of his hand-me-down shirt like a long hairy brown twig. He turned in a circle, taking in the fields to either side and behind the island on which he now stood. "Your Aththa will let me do anything I want with this land. He gave it to me. His son. His oldest son! I am the heir." And he pointed to himself, his mouth turned down, this time with pride.

"Can we come now?" I asked, feeling the need to distract him from dwelling on inheritance, which had proved, in our house, to always lead to tears and accusations on the part of some otherwise sober adult.

"You wait there until I check the place out. I haven't come here for a long time. Avindra, you look after the little ones, okay? Till I come back?"

I turned to look at my oldest brother. I didn't think he was capable of looking after us. Even then my guess was that he was far better at providing us an example, of dispensing advice, of sometimes translating the numerous dictates of our Buddhist philosophies, or singing to us, than he would be at warding off danger from any quarter. His was a jujitsu kind of engagement with the world, a conscious choice to deflect and redirect and sometimes absent himself rather than the head-on tae-kwon-do assaults that were called for by our cultural predilections.

The other brother, though, the middle child, stood straight and alert: he could navigate any waters. By then he had already picked up the speech patterns and concerns of the land-deprived peasants, the up-country estate laborers, the factory workers in the free-trade zones, and, most importantly, my father's politics. He gave speeches and amazed the working classes, whose representatives were omnipresent in our lives and equally reliably silent, as they were required to be. If we needed help from someone in these parts, I was sure he could summon it.

But managing actual threats, from water-dwelling creatures, lizards, or the snakes who lived inside anthills, or even, for that matter, large humans, for those things, they needed me. For wasn't it I who checked on the night noises that made us jumpy when our parents were away? Wasn't it I who fought the actual battles with people, shouting and stamping and scowling until our adversaries, whatever boy or girl had crossed our paths—usually my path—had wilted away?

"Let's go," I said, and clambered to the top. My brothers followed. We couldn't see Loku Māma, nor could we hear him.

"He must have gone to the other side," my oldest brother said.

"He'll be back soon. This island is not that big," the second brother offered.

"Better not follow him, though. He'll get mad," I said.

"We don't have to worry. We know this island," my second older brother said. "Let's split up and find kottamba." We wandered away on cue like little ripples set off by an unseen pebble dropped into our center.

That variety of wild almond was hard to find and even harder to eat, so the pleasure must have come from the exercise rather than the taste. By the time our black heads were almost too hot to touch from walking in the sun, we gathered in the shade of a mango tree to share our finds.

"I got masang," my oldest brother said, opening his palms to reveal the peach and pink fruit.

"Where's your kottamba?" the other brother asked.

"I didn't find any."

"Masang is better," I said, officiating as usual. "We can have it as dessert!"

"Well, nobody told me we were looking for masang. I found ma-sang, too, but I thought we were looking for kottamba."

I coated my voice with the ineffably calming quality it usually found hard to display having such little practice in the art. Among boys, in my experience, there was only room for my just-as-good-and-often-better-than-you-are boy skills. I used to listen with fascination to my grandmother, who drifted in and out of my grandfather's orbit making suggestions that were seemingly addressed to an absent third party and were never in direct reference to the topic at hand—firing the watcher, for instance, or the price of the large fish that my grandfather preferred—almost all of which appeared to end to her satisfaction. How did she manage it? Would I ever find out? More importantly, what was it that gave her great joy? For that, too, was just as obscure. Whether she felt it, desired it, or missed it.

"If you brought masang, too, then we would have too much. We would get sick. You can't eat too much masang, that's what Aththa said." I told my second brother now, who still looked annoyed. "Anyway, you have the most kottamba. See? Even I only got five and you have eleven!"

He smiled the smile that often made him look younger than I was, and pointed back the way he had come. "There's a lot over there. That's how I got them."

"I'll get a stone," I said.

"Get three," my oldest brother advised.

It took a long time, as I recall, for us to finish this repast. First, each kottamba pod, a small, puffy oval about two-thirds the length of a little finger, had to be held just so, so it could be hit repeatedly with a rock without also hurting our own hands. Then, the last strike had to be made with just enough force to reveal the kernel within but not so hard as to shatter it; shattering meant picking off tiny particles of the yellowy-white seed and there was no way to do that without also being forced to taste the sour fibers of the pod itself. Our count was usually fifty-fifty. Half of them would be whole, half a mess. But that day we didn't care, because when it was over, there was masang to follow, an easy fruit.

"I think we should go and look for him," my oldest brother said, after we had consumed the last masang and after my other brother and I had continued to sit there pretending to be busy, piling empty kottamba pods in one corner, our stones on top of one another and then in a triangle, and so forth for a little longer, delaying the inevitability of having to locate Loku Māma and cope with whatever mood he had worked himself up into.

This time we walked in a row, in birth order. I brought up the rear. I don't know how the island got to be so large, bigger than it had ever been to us when we had visited it alone. Now, with Loku Māma missing, it seemed endless and treacherous. How had I missed the caves made by the piles of large rocks at its summit? Even the tall grasses and fruitless coconut trees had escaped my notice. In the distance we could hear the sound of the coconuts falling, brought down by the pluckers who either stood on the ground and sent their knife-topped poles into the trees marked for harvest or shimmied up the branch-bare trunks, miraculously aided by a band of cloth looped around their ankles. But here, there were no pluckers. Why didn't these trees produce any fruit?

"Stop staring and hurry up!" my second brother yelled. I ran to catch up.

"Where do you think he went?" I asked. "There's nowhere to go from here except to the fields. To get back to the main estate, he has to go the way we came, and we would have seen him."

"Maybe he fell somewhere," my oldest brother said, "or maybe he sat down to rest and fell asleep."

We speculated as we walked, our ideas sometimes bordering on hilarity, sometimes verging on such possible tragedy that it made us quiet for a few moments. And maybe it was the very fact that

we had entertained almost every eventuality that made us so un-
prepared for the one we had not thought of: Loku Māma, neck
deep in a pool of water between the two fields behind the island.
A wiry, muscled man, sun darkened to a vigorous deep, wearing
red-and-white underwear several sizes too tight for him and nothing else, was standing by it, urinating and spitting into the water,
laughing.

"Stop that!" I shrieked, and then my trump card: "I'll tell!"

The man finished peeing with a thrust of his hips, the urine almost hitting my uncle in his face where he stood, weeping with rage
and, we all knew it, fright. Then he snapped the elastic of his underwear and swiveled to face us.

"Tell whom? That naaki vesi who owns the land?"

To hear my grandmother referred to as the old whore was one
thing; to learn that it was she, not my talkative grandfather, who
owned the land was another. I couldn't decide which of these was
worse.

"Putha," Loku Māma blubbered, his body gusted by the muddy
water, "don't . . . say . . . anything. You leave these children alone!"
he said to the man.

"Filthy rich brats. You think you own this land? My ancestors
have farmed this land for decades now. My grandfather planted
most of those coconut trees. This land should belong to me!" He
bounced both his fists off his own chest and he spat again into the
water.

"This is our grandfather's land," my oldest brother said. "Please
go away now."

"Please go away now," he mocked. "And what if I stayed?"

"I know whose son you are," my other brother spoke up. "If you
say one more word, I will make sure that the entire village knows
what you did here. By tomorrow your father will not be working
at any of these estates."

The man stared at my brother, his eyes full of hatred. For the first time, I realized that there were things I could tell and things that I could not, no matter how much the truth burned into my body, no matter what justice I felt was deserved. For the first time, my grandfather's land was complicated by people who weren't family and weren't glad to simply exist on the fringes of our needs, for fresh mangoes, for warm food, for the management of lost reptiles and the flapping of mosquitoes. For the first time I hated somebody and it was this man with his bare body, crude language, and lack of fear.

He spat once more on the ground and cursed us. He lunged threateningly toward us, stamping his feet, and snickered when we all moved back, my brothers closing ranks in front of me. Then, he turned and ran. I picked up a stone to throw after him, but my oldest brother caught my hand in midair.

"Don't," he said. "Let him go."

Not that my stone would have hit him anyway. I threw it furiously to the ground. "I hate him," I said.

"I know. But he has reason for how much he hates us," my brother said. My oldest brother was like my grandmother that way. He said things that I didn't always understand until I looked back. I let his remark go untended. Instead, I turned, and we all watched the man run through the fields until he was out of sight. It was like an apparition had disappeared when he was gone, the way the fields moved with the breeze again, the way the sun shone determinedly on us all, the way the return of our previously unharmed surroundings now seemed scarred irreparably by something we could no longer see. We walked down to the water's edge, to where my uncle still stood.

"Come out of the water," my oldest brother said, stretching his hand out to Loku Māma and getting his feet wet in the process. My uncle did not move toward him and my brother waded in farther, trying to be close enough to touch my uncle's hand when he eventually put it out. But he wouldn't come. He shook his head, weeping. I couldn't have known then what those tears were made of, but I knew they were different. They were not miserable, or angry, or impotent, like all the other times. It was more as if the mud-filled paddy water in which he was standing had seeped into his body through the pores of his skin and, having saturated him, was now returning back to the earth through his eyes. He didn't even put up his hands to wipe his face.

"Malli," my brother said, calling to my other brother. "Here, hold my clothes." They were both wearing khaki shorts and blue-and-white checked shirts. My mother always dressed my brothers alike: it was easier to buy a double shirt length than it was to buy them separately, she said. He removed the shirt, the shorts, and his white Bernard's underwear and tossed them, one at a time, to my second brother. I took them from him and folded them neatly, not knowing how else to contribute to the moment. When I held the clothes, it struck me that the man had put on my uncle's underwear and that my uncle was naked in the pool. I started to tell my brother why Loku Māma wouldn't come out of the water, but when I turned to him, my brother had already reached our uncle. The water was not as deep as I had thought if my brother could stand in it; my uncle had to be kneeling.

"Don't cry, Loku Māma," I called out, my voice sounding useless. "Loku Aiyya will help you to come out."

But he simply shook his head. Not even my brother's voice, so calm, so unhurried and devoid of urgency, could make him move. Next to me, my second brother stripped down, leaving his clothes in a heap, and went into the water. I didn't fold them; there was no use pretending all was well. Perhaps that was all he needed, two boys to hold him up. Or maybe the words my brothers were murmuring to him, soothing even to me, though I couldn't distinguish what they were saying, gave him strength. I thought my uncle would care that he was naked, that I was standing there, watching him being dragged out of the water, so limp, so like some large bit of vegetation, a weed even, but he didn't. He stood up, still leaking water from his eyes, silky brown water sliding off his skin, and made his way back to the edge of the pool, leaning as he did with equal weight on my two brothers.

He had always needed us, our uncle, but never with such clarity. Embarrassed and frightened, I walked away to look for his clothes. The shirt lay balled up and wet, quite close to the pool of water. His trousers had been tossed into the branches of a guava tree. I had to climb partway up to retrieve them. His white undershirt was completely covered in mud, so I left it there. My brothers helped him into his trousers and then asked me to stand next to him while they put their own clothes on.

"I'll squeeze the water out of the shirt, Loku Māma," I said. "When we climb back on the island, there's a place with lots of rocks. We'll dry it there for you."

He didn't say anything. He was still sobbing, but quietly, like a child at the end of a long bout of crying. Like children at funerals who know something has been lost but are not sure what it might be. When I had finished squeezing out the shirt, I took his hand and led him over to my damp brothers. We climbed back up the island without further conversation, simply holding out hands, as needed, to help one another up.

"Loku Māma, you can sit in the shade while the shirt dries," my second brother suggested. "Here, by the mango trees." He dusted a flat stone lying nearby and directed my uncle to it. Loku Māma sank onto it without fuss.

I found a smooth spot on the rocky hill we'd passed earlier and spread the shirt on it, inside out, the way my grandmother had taught me. When I returned, Loku Māma was alone.

"Where are they?" I asked, not really expecting a reply.

"I don't know, Putha," my uncle said. He turned up both of his hands, the weak fingers stretched out and curving halfway up as though he were checking leather balls for a game of cricket. "Your Loku Māma doesn't know. You are by yourself now. All of you. I can't help you. I can't help you anymore." And he began to cry again.

"Don't cry," I said, "I'm still here. You are not alone. Don't cry." I said those words because there was nothing else I could think of to say. My faith in my brothers was intact: they would return and there was a reason for their absence. But I couldn't convince him that he was still an adult, still to be depended upon. The fantasy we had allowed him was over. I noticed how bony he was, his rib cage visible beneath the hairy chest that protruded above, small muscles on the arms that lay crossed over his knees, all of his body just barely organized into a full-grown human being. Anything could spread the pieces of him around, scatter his limbs, and splinter his torso, and he would be gone, not as a dandelion might disperse, floating away in grace, but like a meatless bone chewed by an old hungry dog. I stroked his head and repeated myself. "I'm here. Don't cry, Loku Māma."

My brothers came back a little later, their palms filled with masang and kottamba and a few small wild guavas. Where had they found a fruit-bearing tree on this pretend estate willed to my uncle? How far had they dared to go in the wake of what we had witnessed? What did it matter? It occupied us all, the preparing and sharing of that fruit. At first he refused to eat any of it, but eventually he accepted a guava and then some slivers of wild almond, spitting out the stray pith that found its way into his mouth. When we were done, I fetched the shirt, crumpled but dry, and buttoned it on him while he sat. He didn't bother to tuck it in. It looked far too festive on his body, that red. It reminded me of untidy things, like red shoeflowers, crimped and curled. A red shoeflower impaled at the top of a bare brown branch.

I thought of that all the way back to where my grandparents waited, outside the watcher's hut, supervising the counting of the coconuts. We could hear the counting from across the road, the steady rhythm of coconuts being flung, one at a time, from a pile at one end of the swept, sanded midula to a pile on the other. So steady that it seemed it would never cease, the dull smack of the unhusked coconuts, followed by the numbers being called out by the watcher. I knew that my grandmother was keeping track, writing down the figures in hundreds in a notebook in her convent-perfected handwriting. I knew that my grandfather, dressed entirely in white, was alert, beside her, double-checking her figures. I knew that they expected that some portion of the coconuts had already been hauled away and sold by the watcher for his own gain, before they could get there. That was the price of being landed aristocracy: a certain degree of theft was allowed to go on without comment. I knew all this, but I did not know what would happen to Loku Māma and to us children who had rescued him from the terrible burden of witnessed humiliation.

"We won't tell Aththa and Aththamma, will we?" I asked my oldest brother, leaving Loku Māma behind and running ahead a little to catch up to where my brothers were walking, both with their heads bowed.

"No, there's no need to tell them," my oldest brother replied.

"Then what will we do?" I asked.

"Nothing," my other brother said. "There's nothing we can do."

"But you said you would tell the village!" I said, feeling the event slipping away from our grasp, turning from significance to silence.

"The villagers don't want us here either," he said. "They want to own the land."

"Then they should buy some," I said. "They can't take our land. This is our land. This is Aththa's land."

My brothers said nothing. Loku Māma had caught up to us.

"Putha . . . ," he began, addressing my brothers only this time, "your grandparents . . . what happened . . ."

"We're not going to tell them, Loku Māma. You don't have to worry," my oldest brother said. "We'll say that you jumped in to get Nangi out of the water and that's how you got dirty."

"I'm not wet!" I protested.

My brothers glanced at me. "We'll tell them that I fell in," my second brother said, "and you helped us out."

Nobody said anything else the rest of the way.

The story was greeted with concern and a large allocation of blame directed at our uncle.

"Asoka, we have told you not to take these children all over the place. You can't manage them. You can't manage yourself!"

Loku Māma pouted and frowned but remained silent. After a few rounds of protests filled with precise details as to how our uncle had rescued my brother, and how glad we had been for his help, all of which ended invariably with the same reprimands toward Loku Māma, we gave up and said no more.

On the way back from the estate the rains came down. Once we got home, we children were allowed to bathe in the back garden, splashing in the wealth of water collected in the barrels placed under the gutters, sticking our heads under a spout that protruded from the kitchen roof.

"Get all that dirt off yourselves," my grandmother said, "especially the mud from the fields." She sent Seela, the servant girl, for three towels and a cake of kohomba soap for us to use.

Loku Māma sat next to our grandmother on a bench in the back veranda and watched us as he usually did, but without the instructions he had called out on other occasions: *don't slip, watch the edge of the barrel, there's thunder in the distance, come in.* We pretended not to notice.

We didn't forget that day. It simply retired behind our daily lives but for the almost imperceptible alteration of our relationship to Loku Māma. He became more willing to run errands on our behalf rather than the other way around. He continued to take care of us when help was requested by one of our parents, but we all knew it was a charade based on the difference between the height of his body and the smallness of ours. We washed his plates and clothes and ironed his shirts and even fetched his slippers and took away his empty teacups, but we did these things of our own accord, not because he asked, and when we did, he simply bent his head farther into his chest. He didn't flash his old sheepish grin in thanks; he seemed more often than not ashamed that we had even volunteered our services.

We didn't return to the island, and we didn't discuss what had happened there until our grandfather passed away one night. He died without fuss, except for the sound of tears when my grandmother brought him his tea and found him still in bed, with a peaceful countenance but almost cold. The moment we heard, we three instinctively went to the back of the house and stood there in silence. I knew my brothers were, like me, back on that island, hearing our uncle talk about wills and land, seeing not the relief of tending to what had been passed down but the misery of accepting something soiled.

The altercation broke out the day the ashes were to be collected from the crematorium.

"We should spread the ashes on the land," my aunt announced, before even our mother, the oldest child, had expressed an opinion.

"Appatchi's ashes should return to the place where he was born and raised," our father said. "Back to Nattandiya." That was all he said. My father was usually right. We knew when he was wrong because he offered supporting arguments and repeated himself too many times and on too many occasions.

"Nattandiya is not the place for our father," my aunt declared. "His life was with us; it is Kekunagolla that meant something to him. He left Nattandiya behind when he married Amma. Didn't he, Amma?"

My grandmother, dressed in the white of mourning, sat in her usual seat to the right of the head of the table and kept her peace. That meant she did not agree.

"Amma is too upset to think about these things. That's why we have to do it," my mother's sister continued, after waiting a few moments to give my grandmother a chance to respond.

"Who is in charge of the ashes?" my mother asked, obliquely. As the firstborn child, she had the greater say.

"We are all in charge!" her sister replied. "We are all his children, no matter who was born first and who was born last. He was our father. Even Asoka has a say. Asoka! Come here!"

Loku Māma had always been used like a weight at the butcher shop, tossed into one flat pan or the other when his sisters fought, his role one of adding to a count, not for supplying an independent point of view. I was sent to fetch my uncle, who was hiding out in the front veranda.

"Loku Māma, they're looking for you," I said.

"What for? My father is dead now. What is there to talk about?"

"They're talking about where to put the ashes."

"Ashes should be thrown to the wind," he said, flinging his own arms haphazardly toward the garden. "That's where the ashes should go. My father's ashes should be everywhere." He shrugged. "Dust to dust," he added, some remembered bit of Catholicism from his Saint Anne's primary education coming out.

"Kudamma says the ashes should be taken to the land," I informed him, hoping that he would agree. He had been inconsolable at the funeral, grabbing at the coffin and howling when it shut after the wake, having to be held back by two of my uncles when it was time to lift it out of the house. In the end my father had calmed him down by insisting that he shoulder the front left of the coffin while his estranged brother, our other uncle, carried the right. My father had stood behind Loku Māma and had a hand on his shoulder all the way to the kanatta where the body was to be cremated.

But he did not agree. My uncle leaped to his feet and charged into the dining room where the others were sitting. "My father's ashes cannot go back to the land!" he screamed. "I won't allow it!" And in an instant he was the shaking, angry man he sometimes became, his right shoulder jerking forward from his thrusting half-bent frame, his pointing finger, the spit that alternately foamed and flew as he yelled. I went over to my brothers and added myself to their clump.

Everybody but my grandmother rose to their feet. Some of my other aunts hustled our younger cousins out of the room and ear-shot. We three oldest grandchildren stood our ground. My aunt began to berate Loku Māma, accusing him of making a spectacle of himself at the funeral and now causing more grief in a household brimming with it.

"Let him have his say. He has a right to an opinion," my father said. He was the only one still sitting down at the breakfast table with my grandmother. He removed the tea cozy and poured her more tea from the white ceramic pot. She held the cup with one curved palm and watched him add milk and sugar and stir it. She didn't drink it, but she held it close.

"Asoka, we are not saying that the ashes will be only on the main estate. We will spread it equally on all the fields, even in yours," my aunt said.

That was when my uncle picked up the knife and lunged at my aunt. Other adults moved toward him trying to wrest the knife from him, but he was waving it in the air and nobody could get close enough. Swipe, swipe, swipe. A curtain ripped. The fridge got scraped. Another aunt, the youngest of them, yelped in pain. In the end all they managed to do was to back him into the kitchen. My aunt had to hold the doors shut while Loku Māma raged from within.

There is language for anger and there is language for grief. When the two combine, there is no room for politeness. Only curses remain: at family, at the gods, at the dead. My uncle found new lucidity in the kitchen, as he screamed and wept and sharpened and sharpened his knife.

"It's okay," my aunt sobbed. "You can take all the ashes! You can take all the ashes and spread them on your land!"

"Move away from that door!" my mother told her.

"I'm calling the police," the other uncle said in lieu of help.

"I don't care if he cuts off my hands. Just leave my children alone!" my aunt wailed.

My brothers and I exchanged glances. Loku Māma hadn't threatened her children. Loku Māma never threatened the children. All his problems were with the adults.

"Send that old bitch in here!" Loku Māma screamed from inside. "I'm going to kill her and kill myself! Then we can join him!" We could hear him throwing pots onto the floor. We could hear the clay pots shattering, the metal ones bouncing off walls.

"Let's go around to the window," my second older brother said. We slipped out of the dining room, through the front porch, and around the side garden until we were at the window.

"Loku Māma! Loku Māma! Loku Māma!" we called, but softly so only he could hear. Our presence didn't seem to register at first. Loku Māma's face remained blank. He stared at us, the knife dull in his hands except for the edge he had just sharpened, which shone silver in the relative darkness of the kitchen. Beyond him, the only other things that strived to be seen, and were, were the knuckles of my aunt's hands, gripping that door. Having attracted his attention, it seemed none of us could think of what else we could say. In the absence of his screaming all we could hear was our aunt crying about land, about her dead father, and about his ashes.

"Loku Māma, put down the knife," my oldest brother said, and his voice was neither soothing nor unkind. His voice was firm and compassionate like that of our mother tending to one of our wounds; it was a necessary voice.

"We'll ask our Appatchi to tell them to spread the ashes here, on this land," my other brother said. "They always listen to him in the end."

That was true. My mother's family eventually came around to my father's way of thinking. And if anybody could find a way to end this impasse, surely it would be our father. Loku Māma put the knife down and came over to the window. With his hands clutching the bars on his side, and our three sets of fists on ours, we stood looking up at him, and him looking down at us. He seemed half-mad. I wondered what we looked like to him. Did my brothers and I seem as small as I felt? I tried my best to think of something to say, something special and useful like my brothers had done. But all I could think of was fruit trees. All I could think of saying was "the trees on the island have fruits on them." And I didn't know if that would upset this equilibrium we seemed to have found, balancing quiet between him and us on either side of the kitchen window, so I didn't say it.

Then he spoke. It was the first time he had ever sounded like an adult to me. "You three must take care of me now," he said, just before the door behind him opened, cautiously.

I could see the faces on the other side, all the aunts and uncles, the one aunt still crying, another holding her bruised hands in her own, some moving backward away from the kitchen and others forward into it. I could not see my grandmother or my father. With my brothers beside me, I felt strong.

Fault Lines

Mira

She crosses the street, comes up to me, bold as a rabbit in predator-purged territory, ferret-like herself, well-trained suburban calling card on a leash beside her, and asks me—right in front of all the other mothers—if I'm looking for more work as a nanny. The other women have already recoiled, not from her, so much, as from the response they now know to expect from me, their one (fill in your chosen blank) friend. Perhaps at some primeval level they feel sorrier for her than horrified for me. It's too early, even for me. I choose clarity.

—Did you feel entitled to ask me that because I'm the only brown person standing here?

My daughters press against my body on either side, comprehending only its hardness, the chain mail that descends, the armor tossed as though from the hands of a benevolent deity, all haste and consternation as he rushes through neighborhoods intuiting coming events, casting shadows in each set of eyes that hood, each set of lips pursing its contents, the look that is turned inward, asking: Is this it? Is this time for The Crazy Black Man/Woman or is there some mitigating element that must be considered? Time of day? Circumstance? A wrinkle or a smile? What other pressing duty calls that cannot now be derailed with a reaction or a rant? I feel their arms wrap, one higher, one lower, around my thighs, feel the pale strength of them, and do not move my own arms, crossed, waiting, face-off. Silence, and then the chug of the yellow bus coming up the road toward us, its sunshine color stippled by the old oaks that arch overhead and touch each other the way we neighbors will never do. She steps off the street and onto the pavement beside us, lingers there, lost in the shuffle of rituals in which she has no part, while we hustle our children inside and break into our directional cliques, leaving.

—I cannot believe.

—What nerve.

—Are you okay?

Ah, the vernacular of suburbia where we reserve our epithets for colleagues at workplaces where most of us are overpaid, for politicians we imagine give a damn about our vote, and for grouped people—the "those" of our stories—all the absent ones who need never feel nor fear our low-motility seeds of wrath. In the day-to-day, though, that's a different kettle of gefilte, that's a farce called civility, where the only people hurting are the ones who are hoping you might say *fuck*, just once, on their behalf. You're the one wearing whiteface, after all. Fuck you, fuck off, fucking moron, any of those would do. I don't need the potluck or the block party, just give me one flying fuck. Say it loud and clear.

I'm the last mother to reach her house, the farthest from the stop. The chatter of the Friedman toddlers catches up just as I reach my door, and I glance back for a moment to watch the double baby carriage making its vertiginous climb up the slope toward me. I make eye contact with the woman who shares no facial features with her four wards, but I can only manage a commiserating grimace. I've got my own grievance to nurse today.

Iris

Iris Jones works down the street at the house with the sagging gutters and the haphazardly tended garden, where the remains of the last tree felled are still being carted away, a few small logs at a time, by the neighbors who have begun to use their outdoor firepits as they watch the first bulbs bloom along the edges of their own flower beds. There are six children there to fill up the three bedrooms of the house, the fifth still swaddled and kept beside his mother, who is pregnant with the last. Iris manages the older four, all girls, aged six, five, three, and two. They are well behaved and expectant of an excess of attention in all aspects of their lives from baths to play to reading to naps, which they take religiously from one to three each afternoon.

Iris arrives by six in the morning. On the way to the bus stop, she passes Geraldo's Laundromat (where someone has pulled off various letters so it now reads Geraldo's Lat), two shops with wigs on display in colors that God never intended for human heads, and a salon with the "Nails" sign illuminated whether it is open or closed. As she walks to the stop at Ridge and Susquehanna, she thinks about the fact that the prayers from four churches—Church of God of Prophecy, Jones Tabernacle AME Church, Bethel Presbyterian Church, and Faith Emanuel Baptist Church—always surround her as she stands within sight of her sons' high school, waiting for the 61. Each morning, just before the bus arrives, she turns toward the school and bends her head as she mentally gathers the prayers of all four churches to help keep her children safe until she returns. She boards the bus and nods to the same eleven people already sitting in their preferred places—only one, a teenage girl, chooses the aisle—then changes to the 65 at the Wissahickon Transportation Center and tries not to fall asleep before her stop at Bryn Mawr and City Line. It takes her five hundred and seventy-two steps from there to reach the house on Upland Terrace. She lets herself in and hangs up her coat on the metal rack near the ketubah, which, according to the translation offered to her by Chana, tells the world that Yitzak Friedman and Chana Salzburg were married on the twenty-fourth of July, 2009. Every morning Iris does the same math and shakes her head, then changes the motion to a nod because Yitzak is always watching her from the dining table where he is already sitting down, drinking coffee, and reading The Holy Book. In the kitchen that she is allowed to use, she makes herself a cup of tea and a slice of toast, and sets out breakfast for the children, each according to their taste: melon and yogurt for Acimah, banana and yogurt for Arashel, soft buttered white bread with the lightest touch of peach jam for Astera, and oatmeal for Aaliyah.

Upstairs, she wakes each one with soft words or stern, as required, and gets them washed, brushed, and dressed in time for them to kiss their father goodbye before he walks out of the house, still carrying The Holy Book, and, as far as Iris can tell, intending to do so all day long wherever he goes, as he does, each day, on foot. By the time their mother comes down, slowly, slowly, holding the banister with one hand, her baby clutched in her other arm, Iris has prepared breakfast for her and turns her back and does the dishes while Chana nurses her baby and feeds herself. Iris cleans and dresses the baby—and for the baby Iris has soft words and baby songs in unfamiliar yet melodious rhythms—while Chana gets dressed.

At around eight thirty in the morning Iris pushes a double stroller down the middle of the street, the five- and six-year-olds tagged on either side like long ribbons, and refuses to move for cars no matter how long and how hard they toot their horns, or how much their drivers yell out their windows. The ladies at the bus stop roll their eyes at her because Iris's stroller, arriving on its unpredictable schedule, delays the departure of the school bus, though the Jamaican bus driver with the wild hair who drives both the kindergarteners and the high schoolers—and who insists that the boys in both groups first wait until the girls have finished boarding, and then stop and greet him before they proceed to take their seats, quirks that generate smiles from the younger and half smiles from the older—never seems to mind waiting for Iris's progress down the road, which makes the mothers at the bus stop turn and gaze, like choreographed bit-part players in a drama where all of them tried and none of them made the leads, at Iris, and they cannot help but notice her stunning derriere, so they redo their ponytails and adjust their fitted baseball caps and blow extra-special kisses at their wee ones already distracted and otherwise engaged with the particular hierarchies arranged to terrify those consigned to riding public school buses. Only Mira smiles at Iris, though Iris remains oblivious to this virtual high five as she wends her way toward the Bala Cynwyd Library, her thoughts on matters far more pertinent to her day-to-day than the shape of her ass or the politics of her audience.

By the time she is boarding the 65 for her return home, Iris has chalked up between twelve and sixteen thousand steps, which might have registered on her Fitbit or her iPhone if she possessed either one, but which register only on her veined calves, tight and raised like thin vagrant snakes. Iris also works until after dinner on Saturdays because on those days the Friedman family observes Shabbat and the laws of Halacha and would sit hungry in the darkness if not for her. Since she cannot leave until the ritual havdalah is completed, Iris has come to associate the sour-sweet smell of wine and smoke and cinnamon with her long-awaited single day of freedom. On Saturdays the children are whiny and difficult because they are managed entirely by their parents in a routine neither side of the equation recognizes or enjoys. (This does not make Iris feel special or loved.)

Before leaving her house in the Strawberry Mansions neighborhood of Philadelphia, she wakes up her son Diem, sixteen.

—Baby, it's five, I've got to go now. Wake your brothers at six. You be home right after school.

—Okay, Mom. Lock the door.

Then he goes back to sleep and doesn't wake until six thirty and has to scream his brothers awake and through their cornflakes and milk (if there is milk, dry if there isn't), and race out of the door to their school, which is just far enough that they are tired by the time they reach it, but too close for them to qualify for busing. If there are blues out, they have to slow to a stroll, which makes them late and gets them face time with teachers and the vice principal but never the principal, who has too many fires to put out to be bothered with these four smoldering pieces of coal. No matter how frantic their morning becomes, or how late they are—not even that time he had to piggyback his youngest brother, Ozzie, all the way to school because he tripped right outside their door and bloodied both knees, or even the time that his second youngest brother, Jayjo, refused to go to school because he had not studied for his English test and swore that Mr. Bomze hated him and Diem had to drag Jayjo out and cuff his head and force march him until he was within sight of the first teacher—Diem never forgets to stop and lock the door.

Gabriella

You never think that things will turn out as badly or as well as they do. When you turn sixteen and you have no boyfriend and you are not pregnant and everyone says—yes, even Abuela, who has had you pegged as a malparida since you were seven years old and lifted your dress in front of the whole school while singing the national anthem—that you've beaten the odds and broken the family tradition of being knocked up before your quinceañera, you want to believe it. You stroke your flat belly and then you go and get one of those diamond-dust studs put in your navel, the type that has the thin dangling gold chain that points toward your not-available cuca, because you want to show it off. How off limits you are, how you are not like the rest of the Roman sisters, or your mother, or your aunts, particularly not Titi Maria, who was pregnant at fourteen—fourteen!—or even your grandmother. The thing is, you put a sweet chain like that, which cost all your quinceañera money, in your belly button, your sweet diving-pool belly button, and the only thing you want to do is make sure everyone can see it. So you stop listening to the family chorus and you wear nothing but crop tops and low-rise shorts and jeans, and skirts with the waist rolled down, and you are just like all the stupid girls with tats that you scorned because oh my God they carved the names of boyfriends and hearts between their breasts and on the skin over the angel-wing bones on their backs and were never after seen in real clothes, only T-back tops and V-necked shirts that were not T-shirts, who were they kidding, they were ho halters.

Ricardo said it was the jewelry in your middle that made him love you so much. That made him love you and bump into you in the hallways so he could see how the gold chain swung against your beautiful skin like a pendulum. So what if you had to spend junior year sitting sideways at your desk and pretending you don't notice Mr. Bomze staring at your ballooning chest all through English class, and you had to take the diamond-dust stud and its gold chain out, and you didn't get to graduate because whatever hell that felt like, Luis is fifteen and Ricardo still treats you like you were already born a princesa before he made you his queen with all of that loving.

And now, after all these years, you might even get a nursing certificate or something in the medical field that you could use from the Philadelphia College of Osteopathic Medicine, which is around the corner from your job, so close that you could go there after work. That's what Iris said when she handed you the brochure that she had brought home from the library near where she works. At first you had laughed because those brochures were not there at the library near where Ricardo works at the high school and where you have waited for him on the evenings when he's taken you to watch Luis run at the track meets—and you love watching Luis run because his feet move as though God himself has taught him how to walk on air, but you don't mention this part to Iris because none of her boys can run—though both libraries belong to the same district and maybe, you joked, it was because that library was filled with morenos just like the community swimming pool near there, and maybe nobody wanted to encourage those people to go back to school. But Iris did not laugh. She just said, You got your GED, now give them a call. It's time.

And you felt sorry and made a tray of asado de puerco for her to take home because even though her boy Diem had also applied for the same program, only Luis was accepted and now Luis lives at the ABC house, not too far from where you both work. He's learning to tread water, he says, at the private pools of his friends' homes in the better neighborhoods because he goes to their school now, where he has a brand-new MacBook Pro computer for free like all the other students, plus tutors and special attention because he is going to be A Success Story. That is what the program director told you when you hugged Luis and cried when you had to leave him there and go home.

Of course Abuela scoffed. They want to take my boy (she calls

Luis her boy even though you were the one who gave birth to him and she was so disappointed in you that she still only speaks indirectly to you), they want to take my boy and put him in the rich people's school so they can show off how rich schools can help poor kids? Why not give some of that money to his school so all the kids in the school can have what they have?

And you want to explain to her, the way the program director had explained to you, that it was not just money in poor schools but the *environment* that made the difference, that your community and your family and your general *trajectory* were what held kids like Luis back, but you couldn't get your tongue adjusted around all those words. So you don't say anything, because you know she'd just say ¡Vete a la mierda! and make you feel stupid for having had the nerve to address her, but also because Ricardo is looking at you with that *I told you so* gleam and sucking his back teeth, so you just do the same and look away because you agree. You agree that there was nothing wrong with your community and your family and your trajectory. You got pregnant and you did the right thing and so did Ricardo and you got married and you had both always done the best you could for all your children. And if you were asked, you'd even say you were doing your best for theirs because how would Mira keep her job that takes her all over creation doing God knows what, and how would Ari (which is short for Aristides) keep his, which pays not only for his second family but also for his first, which comes with not one but two daughters in college on the other side of the country and a son and don't even get you started on the first wife who drives the car with the top rolled down every time she pulls out of her double driveway two doors from her ex-husband's house, the one she bought—so Mira says—just to spite him.

It makes you happy-sad-angry to hear about all the wonderful teachers, most of whom are male, in the school that Luis goes to over past City Line Avenue, when neither Rosita nor Rickey Junior have teachers like that because they still go to the school that Diem and his brothers do on this side, and the only male is the principal who is a hijo de puta who always stares at your chest and tells you how pretty Rosita is. You stay silent and you think that maybe they, too, will get to go to the other school and live in a house with tutors and all you can do is pray that they'll last, beautiful as they are— with Ricardo's eyes and your mouth and color—without babies to be looked after before they have finished being yours.

Mrs. Petralia, who prefers to be called Mira, is happy to hear that you are going to try to go back to school, though she insists she cannot manage without you because she and Ari are so busy all the time and her children need you.

—Ephie and Athena are so used to you being here when they come home from school, Gabby. How will we manage without you?

—The girls are old enough now, they will be all right.

You say that and it sounds heartless, and you know that it is probably not true—the only person those girls see reliably is you— but what else can you say? You are hoping that Ricardo will be able to find you work in the cafeteria at the middle school, which would pay you more than you make now taking care of the Petralia children and then you could look at all the classes you might need to finish if you want to take this osteopathic medicine business seriously. You'd prefer the high school because then, like Ricardo, you'd get to see Luis every now and again as he walks through the halls or goes to the locker rooms after school to change for track, even if, like Ricardo, you would not wave, or meet his eyes, or in any way acknowledge any relationship even though that would be almost impossible for you, you'd do it, you're sure you would. Still, despite all that longing for what you really want, you know you will take what you can get because, as Iris says, it is time.

But it doesn't work out that way. That's the thing about things never being as bad or as good. Ephie breaks her foot, so you have to keep working and now you have more hours, and enough money so you can call up the school and see what classes you might be able to take there, but too many late nights, which means you obviously cannot enroll at the Philadelphia College of Osteopathic Medicine. It does not sound like the kind of place that would make allowances for students like you. And you tell yourself it's all right. Because the middle school didn't have a vacancy anyway. And you should be paying more attention to Rosita, she is that age, as Abuela keeps saying, and madre de dios you do not want Rosita to have to drop out of school, even the same subpar school you went to, and isn't life like this anyway? And isn't family like this? What does it matter if only one of your children gets to go to the rich people's school, and if only one of you gets to watch your son in these last few years before he leaves home, and if only one of the females in your family finishes high school, when you put it all together, aren't you A Success Story too?

Mira

The next time I see her, I cross the road at the last minute and then I occupy the whole pavement with my stride so that she has to step off, hound and all, her eyes darting away from my stare. For the next few weeks, whenever she sees me on the road, she turns around and scurries back the way she came, her backside all flab and sway in her hurry. It isn't enough for me. Somehow she has crept under my skin and try as I might I cannot find the needlepoint tool with which to pry her out. The needlepoint tool with which to wound her in the precise manner with which she wounded me.

Nanny. It's not that I haven't heard it before, or recognized it in the pass-over looks that I get from the mothers and fathers in this neighborhood. This neighborhood where every mother's son

on a bike appears to be training for the Tour de France, every run-
ner suckling like pigs, hooked up to the breastmilk of ever-present
bottles of water, every new mother doubling as a yogini. At the high
school pool I was asked by a woman, all diamond tennis bracelet
and straw hat, if I, too, was from Jamaica, like her friend's nanny.
I'd had afternoon sex, so I spoke upscale suburban and sailed on
seemingly unscathed. But this one, this canine-led hussy and her
words, just won't let me be. I lie awake at night counting the ways.
I wake up ragged. I walk to the bus stop raring for battle.

Things take time, but if you remain alert, the moment arrives.

Pescatore is still too new for its liquor license, and the fish is
foul, but the wine and desserts are worth the price of admission. I
know the moment I walk in that this is it. There she sits, paramour
or husband beside her, friends and their possessives surrounding.
Here I sit, my own man, my friends and their partners surrounding. Each of us couples brought a bottle—Ari and I, two, since this
had been our idea—and we carried it back out in our bodies. We
all howled with laughter on our way home, drunk in ways that alcohol alone cannot arrange.

We watch her go to the bathroom and hatch the plot right then
and there between getting our check and paying it. We waited
until she had returned from the bathroom. We poured the dregs of
each of our bottles of wine into a glass off which we wiped my lipstick stain, and sent it to her with a note: *Are you looking for more
clients? My friend is also interested. Maybe after dessert?* Definitely
not a paramour. Only a husband in good standing would assume
betrayal, not insult. So it wasn't the *fuck* I so often want to hear
from them, but it'll do; solidarity speaks many dialects.

Gabby has fallen asleep on the couch by the time we get back
and I'm exultant so I laugh her awake, pay her double, and offer her
Ari—still smiling, but also shaking his head, he's too drunk—to
drive her home.

—No, it's all right, gracias, Ricardo will come and pick me up. He doesn't like me getting into another man's car. Even Mr. Petralia.

—It's a long way for him to drive. I can take you. Will he let me drive you home?

On the way back we talk about Ephie, and the injury. I ask her about the College of Osteopathic Medicine, whether she is still hoping to go. She says that she might think about it after her younger son and daughter are out of high school. For now, she'd like to stay close to home to make sure she can keep an eye on them. Her best friend's son was accused of dealing and thrown out of school.

—He didn't do anything. He's like gold, that boy. He takes care of his brothers all day while his mother works at the Friedman house as a nanny. Bad things happen even to the good kids.

—Friedmans? They live down the street? Five kids and the mother is pregnant? That's your friend who looks after those children?

—Iris, yes.

—Iris. I see her taking those children somewhere every morning.

—To the library. Iris likes the library.

—Maybe you should take Ephie and Athena there too?

—For what? Your house has books in every room! Maybe Iris should just bring the children there instead.

She doesn't join me when I laugh. Ricardo opens the door as soon as we pull in to the driveway leading to the flat ranch-style house with its aluminum siding, the tiny square footage of its front yard fenced as though to protect something precious. Gabby calls out that it was only I who drove her back, and he nods and holds the door open for her. I get out of the car to prove my gender, shake his hand. He mentions the time and I feel reprimanded. I tell her to take the day off, that I will stay home with Ephie. The door shuts softly behind them. I wait until the thin porch goes dark and back out without turning on my lights.

Ari is asleep when I get back, the dank smell of alcohol rising from his body. In the cooled stale air of the bedroom, I feel nauseated. I go through the mail downstairs, pick up a few things, make lists, waiting for fatigue to find me. It is nearly dawn by the time I lie down on the couch next to the boxes I've filled with books for Gabby's family. I hope they are age appropriate. I fall asleep between figuring out how to ask the ages of her children and consternation that I do not know. Perhaps Ari does. If nothing else she could share them with her friend Lily, who must surely have a few children of her own.

Iris

He was late for all the same reasons he was late each day, and he was running for all the same reasons he ran each day: he overslept, his brothers dallied, he had to make sure the door was locked.

When Iris got the call on her cell phone, it came from the principal. She dried her hands before she answered. She hung up the phone, finished getting the children dressed, set them at the dining table with coloring books and puzzles, changed the baby—though this morning she had no coos for her and her voice was low but not gentle—washed the dishes, and waited until Chana had finished breakfast to ask her for the rest of the day off.

—What's the matter? Are you sick?

—Yes.

—Is it the flu? Hold on just a minute.

Chana got up and poured four glasses of orange juice, then added Emergen-c into each cup and handed them to her children before returning to the kitchen. Iris leaned against the fridge and waited.

—I feel dizzy and my chest hurts. I need to go home and lie down.

—You can lie down here.

Chana gestured to the living room couch. She looked both concerned and distracted, her mind elsewhere.

—No, I need to go home.

Inconvenience was mentioned, and poor timing. How would Chana get to her mothers' meeting? There was a well-baby checkup later today, too, and now she'd have to postpone it. Was she sure, Chana asked, was Iris certain it wasn't just fatigue? Perhaps a cup of tea, a little sitting down, might help. Hypochondria was suggested. A previous lapse in duty just like this was brought up. That was an illness associated with the personal interview that had been requested by the school guidance counselor after Diem had applied for the ABC program (school conferences and domestic emergencies were never mentioned by Iris). As far as Chana knew—nothing asked, even less volunteered—Iris lived alone and had no family to speak of. Still, when Iris began to wheeze, Chana hurried her out of the house and assured her that she wouldn't dock her a day's pay after all. Whether that registered as a saving grace on Iris, Chana could not tell. (It did not.)

The younger boys were called in to testify that, yes, indeed, they had made their brother late. Additionally, they said, they were often guilty of this because although he woke them up with due diligence at six each morning, they dawdled. It was not his fault. Why had he been running away from school rather than toward it, the blue asked, his belt, buckles, holster, and badge all gleaming and potent.

—I had to lock the door.

And Iris bowed her head, remembering. Once, just once, that door had been left unlocked. And as if he had been waiting all these years, watching the door for just that very day, Susa had come in, sat down, and waited for her to come home. Susa, whom she managed to forget each time she turned away from her boys and their milk-added coffee skin, but only then. Later, after he'd left, she had let her sons out of the room in which their father had locked them, and all night long Diem had tended her bruises. All night, without a single tear on either side, only the silence of alliance and resolve.

She asked, but only a single teacher—Science, a new recruit already harried but clearly still hopeful of great undertakings—spoke on his behalf.

Gabby came with her some evenings to visit Diem. Some days she went alone, or Gabby sent Ricardo. Between the three of them, they did not miss a single day. At first, Iris's younger sons set an alarm and walked slowly and on time to school, but eventually only Ozzie kept trying. He wanted to be able to say that his brother did not have to worry about him anymore. One day, when Diem was allowed to come home. One day.

Gabriella

Your son walks into the house where you work and you say nothing. How could you not have known that somehow this whole thing couldn't work the way it was supposed to? You had done all the right things. You had not gone back after dropping him at the house, you never called him, you waited for him to call you, and when he visited, you did not send him back with the kinds of gifts that you wanted to because you knew he had to cultivate different tastes now and you didn't want to remind him of the things he loved and missed with all his might. You had praised Ricardo each time he came home and said he'd seen Luis and had managed to turn away from your son, giving nothing away. Instead, you had held him close and pretended that it was not longing for Luis but desire for you that was weighing his body down, and you told him again and again that it was best, it was only four years and then you would both have your son back for good.

But then you come back from picking up the girls at the bus stop and you see him sitting at the dining table with Ari's son, and you hear him talking in a way you don't recognize but can't help but admire, and it is not your mouth but your hands that betray you. You cannot help it. You reach out and you stroke his head, and Theo laughs.

And you wouldn't have minded the laugh, you even smiled at the sound of it, withdrawing your hand, folding the memory of that silken hair into your palm as stealthy as a card shark, but then Luis turns and sees you and he swears. He swears at you in language you will never repeat to Ricardo because you cannot break Ricardo's fierce, strong heart that has loved you so well for so long, right from the beginning, words that rise before your eyes and blur as you see them written in letters as big as the ones on the sign outside the Faith Emanuel Baptist Church that you go to each Sunday, the glassed-in one that says in elegant font that Jesus Loves You and that It Is Not Too Late To Repent. And how is it that instead of lifting your hand and striking your son so he can never speak to you again, his shame would be so great, his remorse so bottomless, how is it that you remember to cover Ephie's ears? How is it that you can even think about the fact that Ephie speaks Spanish almost as fluently as your own daughter, not because she has been born with your language ringing in her ears, but because she listens to language tapes that come in shrink-wrapped yellow boxes and spends her summers at camps where they speak to her only in Spanish? How is it that you forget that Theo, too, whose accomplishments were chosen and paid for by the same father, must once have attended those same camps?

You take the girls into the kitchen and you only half listen because what more is there to listen to?

—I can't believe she touched you! My father is fucking crazy to have her around. C'mon, man, let's go over to my mom's house.

And you think about that, about this business of having two houses and two sets of parents and two lives and you wonder if that is what makes people like Mira and Ari happy, the way they can separate what should be inseparable so easily and so neatly, like yolks from whites, and you wonder if Ephie and Athena ever think about that, about how their father once loved someone other than their mother, and whether that bothers them at all. You think about Theo and if he even thinks of Mira as a mother at all. You think about all kinds of things, but you don't think about what Luis has said, or the way the brush of his hair has stained your palm with a feeling you cannot rub out, a feeling you neither want to remember nor forget.

———

At the library Iris picks up two sets of whatever brochures have been set out: for night classes, technical training, online colleges, language instruction, book groups, and summer programs for teenagers that combine sports, reading, and mathematics. She shares them with Gabby.

Iris keeps her set beside her bed and never opens them; they are a decoration.

Gabby flips through her brochures each night, and each night in rotation she pictures a new life that she might make, a life where nothing that should be together is ever pulled apart.

Across the line that divides the city, before turning out the lights for bed, Mira flips through catalogs for clothing complete with backstories, and other frivolities, dog-earing the pages that catch her eye.

Each woman dreams of purchases none of them will ever make. In their various beds, some hard, some soft, differently lonely, their children dream too.

Acknowledgments

These stories have taken the long way home. I am truly lucky to call Julie Barer and Nicole Cunningham my agents—they are as fearless in their critique as they are as champions of the end product. I am equally fortunate in my editors at Graywolf, Fiona McCrae and Steve Woodward; without their quiet persistence these stories would be far less elegant than they are today. And there would be about a thousand more unnecessary coordinating conjunctions!

I am indebted to the many journal editors who requested a story and therefore made me write a new one. Gratitude is also due to people who, by relating a moment from their lives, inspired me to imagine the story that surrounded it.

I am deeply grateful to John Hennessy for encouraging me to put this collection together. Without his frequent enthusiasm for seeing my stories in print, I would not have worked as hard at editing them or indeed gathering them under a single title. I owe you a dedication.

During the pandemic, protests, and lockdowns, my neighbor Sheryl Williams afforded me a safe haven for my heart, my work, and my crazy. Beth Alvarado, Nicole Aragi, Anna Badkhen, Charlie Baxter, Dwayne Betts, Chris Boucher, Michael Collier, Eugene

(BG) Cross, Janet Davis, Richard Ford, John Freeman, Nathalie Handal, Jane Hirshfield, Jamaica Kincaid, Rickey Laurentiis, Pam Loughman, Colum McCann, Ariana Reines, Charles Rice-Gonzalez, George Saunders, Rick Simonson, Pritu Singh-Sampeur, Cheryl Strayed, Jan Swenson, Sarah Taddeo, and TC Tolbert never failed to hold whatever I placed in their hands with care—terrors or joys. Despite the physical distances, you are my come-from-everywhere, messy as all get-out, sometimes divergent, all-American family.

I thank Fiona McCrae a second time here for the gift of her discernment. She embodies the principles most of us lack the courage to embrace, and, by taking the right risks first, she inspired a generation of editors to follow suit. The American literary landscape has been transformed by her wisdom and her impeccable taste. You are an exceptional brilliance whom I call The Goddess for all the right reasons.

I am grateful to my father, Gamini Seneviratne: his daily missives recounting the many accomplishments, talents, and works of my American poet and writer friends remind me that literature still retains the right to travel across borders and quarantines, and to move people on the other side of the world.

My brothers, Arjuna and Malinda Seneviratne, and my sisters-in-law Manju Dharmasiri and Samadanie Kiriwandeniya never let me forget that I live in their sight as their beloved sister. For an immigrant, there is no greater comfort.

Above all, always, the girls at the center of my heart deserve everything I have to give for the mellifluous fanfare they make in and of my life: you are my wishes, my miracles, my I love yous. You are my raison d'être.

To my mother I owe everything. Even now, twelve years on.

RU FREEMAN is an award-winning Sri Lankan and American novelist, poet, editor, and critic, whose work appears internationally and in translation. She is the author of two novels, *A Disobedient Girl* and *On Sal Mal Lane*, a *New York Times* Editors' Choice Book, and the editor of two anthologies, *Extraordinary Rendition: American Writers on Palestine* and *Indivisible: Global Leaders on Shared Security*. She holds an MFA in poetry and an MA in labor studies, researching female migrant labor in the countries of Kuwait, the UAE, and the Kingdom of Saudi Arabia. She has worked at the Institute for Policy Studies in Washington, DC, in the South Asia office of the American Federation of Labor and Congress of Industrial Organizations (AFL-CIO), and for the American Friends Service Committee (AFSC) on social justice initiatives around sanctuary and human rights. She teaches creative writing in the US and abroad and directs the Artist Network at Narrative 4.

The text of *Sleeping Alone* is set in Garamond Premier Pro.
Book design by Rachel Holscher.
Composition by Bookmobile Design and Digital
Publisher Services, Minneapolis, Minnesota.
Manufactured by Friesens on acid-free,
100 percent postconsumer wastepaper.